ALL SOULS ARE FINAL

A VIC VALENTINE FEVER DREAM

BY WILL VIHARO

ALL SOULS ARE FINAL

"All Souls Are Final" originally published by P.I. Tales

"Panty-Stuffed Snakeskin Shoe" originally appeared in the NoirCon
2022 program

Cover art by Dyer Wilk
Formatting by Rik Hall – RikHall.com

ISBN-13: 979-8-218-13117-3

First Printing
Printed in the United States of America

Published by Thrillville Press

www.thrillville.net   www.willviharo.com

To Monica
My Real One and Only

CONTENTS

ALL SOULS ARE FINAL

The Hunter

I really didn't mean to run the guy over. It was an accident or fate, or an accident of fate. But let me back up a bit, so to speak.

Don't take this personally, but generally speaking, I hate people. I'm a misanthrope though I do have selective empathy, particularly for all animals and certain women. The remaining sentient beings in my orbit require effort.

Case in point: the guy who was sitting next to me at the otherwise barren bar, sullen and sulking. I resented his proximity for no good reason, other than he was cramping my style, which is mostly solitary. He was wearing a red hunting cap, flannel shirt and jeans. I am anti-hunting and so I am anti-hunters. He smelled of cheap whiskey which meant he had a head start on his alcoholic high before landing here.

This was about twenty or so years ago at The Drive-Inn, the now long-defunct combination video store/bar/burlesque hall in the Richmond District of San Francisco, owned and operated by Curtis Jackson, better known to the community at large as Doc Schlock. My office was upstairs. Besides my landlord, he was my friend and confidant for many years. I put that in the past tense because he's dead now, though I'm still haunted by his spirit, naturally chalked up to one of my many delusions. I miss when the only spirits that haunted me were the ones Doc poured into my glass as I sat there staring at the exploitation movies playing on the big screen TV. He always listened to my latest woes and offered counsel and comfort. I miss my friend. He was one of the good ones. Humans, I mean.

"Hey, ain't you never show any sports on that thing?" the hunter said. He had a distinctly Southern drawl. I looked over and noticed he was wearing a football jersey beneath the flannel. Dallas Cowboys. I liked their cheerleaders, anyway.

"Never," Doc said. "Sorry."

Cannibal Holocaust was playing, as I recall. It serves the narrative, so I'll go ahead and remember it that way. I was repelled by the few scenes of real animal slaughter, which I always tuned out. The tropical human carnage, which at least seemed just as authentic, went well with Mai Tais. But I was knocking back boilermakers. Doc was no mixologist, so I always ordered my tiki drinks in actual tiki bars.

"What is this trash?" the hunter asked with attitude.

"*Cannibal Holocaust*," I said.

"Looks like something on one of those educational nature shows except it's about people, not just animals."

"Italian cannibal movie. You could say it's a metaphor for how mankind devours his own as a matter of brutal survival, but really, it's just a sleazy exploitation flick.

Probably the most notorious grindhouse movie of all time next to the original *I Spit on Your Grave*."

"Fuck is that?"

"Rape and revenge flick. Gold standard of the genre. The one with the beautiful Camille Keaton. Buster's granddaughter. Or niece or something like that."

"Buster who?"

"Forget it, man. Not your thing."

"Can't you put on something else? This is making me sick. I have a weird history with cannibals. It's a trigger for me."

"I understand that rape is a trigger for many but cannibals? Were you stranded in the jungle or something?"

"I don't want to talk about it. Just change it, please." He seemed more disturbed than annoyed.

Ever the gracious host, Doc popped out the DVD and replacing it with one of my favorites, *The Curious Dr, Humpp*, a sordid but stylish Argentinian sex/horror flick from the sixties, salvaged by *Something Weird Video* in Seattle, where I live now.

"Fuck is this?" asked the hunter after a few scenes of sensual surrealism.

"Art film," Doc said, winking at me.

"What kinda dive is this, anyway?"

"A friendly kind. Here's a free refill." Doc poured the guy another shot on the house. We were both drinking the same brand, Sinatra-sanctioned Jack Daniels, so we had that in common. After Doc reloaded my own shot glass, I offered a toast as a matter of diplomacy. I always prefer to keep the peace because I'm basically too lazy to fight.

"Here's to National Geographic," I said.

The hunter grimaced. "Huh?"

"C'mon, man, next to Playboy, those pictures of naked jungle babes got me through puberty. Best thing about Italian cannibal movies, too."

No audible response. I stared up at the TV screen, but I could feel the hunter's eyes silently judging me. That's okay, I'd already sized him up as a hick anyway. We all judge each other. It's why our faux-civilization is doomed.

"You from here?" he asked abruptly.

"San Francisco? No. New York."

"Figures."

"How come?"

"Big city elite. I can tell. Watch all these weird movies and call 'em 'art films' when they're just trash. You and that black bartender." Doc was in the back, avoiding us, pretending to wash dishes.

The "black" crack only served to confirm my stereotypical first impression. I treaded lightly after that. "Look man, we get all kinds in this town. It's a microcosm of the planet. Where you from?"

"Arkansas."

"Nice."

"You been there?"

"No."

"So, why'd you say that?"

"Just being polite, I guess. I hear good things."

"Like what?"

"I don't know. Lots of trees. I like it green. Not enough

trees around here. I dream of living someplace green."

"Yeah, it's beautiful," the hunter said, drifting inward for an instant. "I miss it."

"So why you here?"

"Got into some trouble back home. Had a buddy over in Oakland offer to put me up, found me in bed with his girl, then he kicked me out."

"Oh. Well, that sucks. Was she worth it?"

He grinned and slapped me on the shoulder. "Ain't they all?"

I smiled and nodded. "In the moment, anyway. So, what now for you? Where to?" Frankly I just wanted him to leave, but meantime I was feigning interest in his plight.

He shrugged. "I don't know," he said sadly.

"Maybe leave the country? Canada? Mexico?"

"What for?"

"I mean, if you really want to escape whatever trouble you're in." I'd immediately assumed it was something illegal. And bad. He just radiated so much sorrow. And tragedy. I could smell it beneath the whiskey.

"No, I'd never leave my country," he said.

"Why not? I'd love to travel. Well, I hate traveling. But I'd love to go to Europe someday. If I could be transported, like on 'Star Trek.' The old one with Kirk."

"I'm a proud American."

"Good for you."

"You're not?"

"I'm not a nationalist. I don't wave flags or join tribes. I'm a lone wolf."

"You sayin' you hate America?"

I'd just accidentally tripped a landmine, so I backed off carefully. "I don't hate it. I love things about it. Like jazz and bourbon and Marilyn Monroe and what passes for freedom nowadays. Some things I don't like, like bigots posing as patriots. Where you're born is just plain dumb luck. How can you be proud of luck?"

"You're not lucky. You need to fight for your freedom. You take it for granted. Those Muslims who took down the towers ain't never gonna quit." Keep in mind this was way back when our terrorists weren't mostly domestic in nature.

"So, join the army, take the fight to them. They're giving away free vacations to Iraq as we speak. Of course, they're working vacations."

"I can't. Not now."

"Oh. Your trouble. I try to avoid trouble and tribes, man, so I dig."

"I don't know what to do."

"Sorry."

"No, you're not."

"You're right. I'm trying hard to care, though."

"Don't hurt yourself. If you were a Christian, you wouldn't have to try."

"I had some Catholic in me until I saw an exorcist."

"Huh?"

"Never mind."

"Yeah, I will never mind. I know your type, all right. I think you're a loser."

"Well, I have no need for your approval, so I really don't care. The opinions of strangers have no impact on my quality of life."

"You got a smart mouth for such a little guy."

"I'm brutally honest by nature, with myself and with others. In both cases, it can cause discomfort. I apologize."

The hunter suddenly stood up, tossed a few dirty dollars on the bar, spat a "fuck you" in my direction, then split. Finally.

Doc came out of hiding. "He gone?"

"Yeah."

"Good. Something about him made me nervous."

"He was dumb but harmless. Like my cat."

"Where'd he go?"

"Beats me. Like I said, he's lost. In both senses"

"He all right?"

"He will be."

"How do you know?"

"I don't. Nobody does."

It was a lazy Sunday. I hadn't had a case in weeks. I was drinking on credit. Paying rent on credit, too. If Doc wasn't my friend as well as my landlord, I'd be a street bum by now. I had no right to look down on anyone. I was always a few bucks away from being totally destitute. Suddenly I felt pity for that stranger.

I finished my beer and a few more shots and decided to head out into the twilight, maybe hit up a whorehouse, one that took credit cards. I was horny and lonely as usual.

I went around back of The Drive-Inn to the private parking lot, fired up my Corvair, and headed out towards Geary. I turned on the radio, always tuned to my favorite station, 960AM KABL. Frankie Laine was singing "That

Lucky Old Sun." Made me smile. Reception was spotty so I adjusted the dial as the car rolled forward slowly towards the intersection without my direct supervision. That's when I felt the impact of the collision. With a body. A human body. One I recognized.

It was the hunter.

This had never happened to me before, except in my most fearful fantasies. I was paralyzed with dread. The hunter had landed on the roof of the Corvair then rolled off. He didn't get up. I looked around. Miraculously, nobody witnessed the actual accident, as far as I could immediately tell. If it was an accident. For all I knew he deliberately walked in front of me. After all, he was in rough emotional shape, not many promising prospects from what he confided, probably on the lam from the law. I didn't want to be a fellow fugitive.

Some pedestrians gathered around. I asked if anybody saw what happened. No takers. A siren wailed close by. Somebody had seen something, obviously, and called the cops.

The patrol car rolled up and I flashed my PI badge as if that gave me diplomatic immunity. No dice.

I didn't touch the prone body but the blood drooling from his mouth on the pavement told me this was not my day. Or his. An ambulance was dispatched as the cops interrogated me. They knew me since I was a regular at the local precinct. I don't think they liked me. The feeling was mutual.

The hunter was pronounced dead at the scene. Turned out he had a name: Hunter. Hunter Thompson. Really.

They gave me a breathalyzer test. I failed, but then I wasn't given time to study. I was fucked. I'd lose my license. All of them. Detective, gun, car. I was out of business, and maybe out of the whole damn rat race, just like that.

If only it were that fucking simple.

The Haunted

Pending further investigation into "the incident" I was released on my own recognizance thanks to a few favors owed me by the proper authorities, meaning the dirty ones who knew I knew they were dirty. I had no real record except for being a pain in their ass. I was deemed legally drunk so a DUI was already on my ledger, not my first, but someone mysterious yet benevolent had called into the station and claimed Hunter the hunter had been suicidal, per personal association. They'd witnessed the accident from a distance and wanted to bail me out, but no need. The call was anonymous, so it didn't really help me out. Right now, the fuzz was trying to track down the one person who could save my ass and the rest of me too.

No one could ever ease my conscience though. I was a wreck, wondering if I'd mowed the sucker down out of subliminal hostility, since as I pointed out I immediately disliked him. When he was alive, that is. Now that he was abruptly dead, he was starting to grow on me.

The newspaper reports of the accident didn't identify

either one of us by name, but since I knew his name from the police report, I did an internet search at the local library. Of course, all I got was stuff about Hunter S. Thompson, the writer. Fear and Loathing in Arkansas didn't seem to be an option. I was curious as hell about this guy now. I like to get to know people before I kill them. Part of my code.

My driver's license had been immediately revoked and my vehicle impounded, of course. But I still had my business and my gun, a .38, at least for now. But without wheels that meant all professional and personal transportation had to be via BART and buses, which severely limited my options. I didn't have any cases pending anyway. It'd been over ten years and I was already burning out. Initially I was only in this racket to find my long-lost love. Instead, she found me. Then I lost her again. I just kept doing this since I wasn't qualified for anything else. Hell, I wasn't even qualified to be a private detective, either. But I was good at faking it. Maybe I should've been an actor. Fate, my pimp, kept supplying me with work.

I was sitting at my desk, nodding off. I hadn't slept at all, so I knew this wasn't a nightmare. Nowadays I take pills to sleep, fuck, and not kill myself.

Mainly I couldn't sleep because I kept seeing Hunter's dead eyes, both before and after I ran him over. Naturally I couldn't stop shaking with self-pity about my own sorry situation. At least his deal was done. He didn't have to worry about anything anymore. Still, I didn't envy him. I just wondered where he went, and if I had inadvertently sent him there, with or without his consent.

The phone rang, jarring me out of my moribund moping. A very female voice asked if I was Vic Valentine.

"The one and only."

"I hear you work for cheap."

"Sometimes I take it out in trade." I shouldn't have said that, but I no longer gave a damn. I was doomed anyway. Plus feeling loopy. These days I'd have been immediately cancelled and put out of my misery.

"I take it you don't mean baseball cards."

"Comic books."

She was already tired of me and cut to the chase. "I want you to find this guy."

"Any guy in particular?"

"I can't say over the phone."

"Okay. Come to my office, we'll talk."

"He's been missing for a few days now. I'm worried."

"I understand."

"I don't know who else to call. I've tried everyone. No one seems to care."

"Why don't you just call the cops?"

"That was plan A. I had to burn through the whole alphabet before I resorted to calling you."

I liked her. Her voice was husky, and she had a way with words. Plus, the idea of taking it out in trade didn't make her hang up on me. "Where are you now? I can come to you." Eventually, via public transit.

"No. I don't want my boyfriend to know. He's with the Hell's Angels."

"Oh, okay." Boyfriend. And a biker to boot. Damn.

"He can't know I'm looking for him."

"You mean the boyfriend can't know you're looking

for this other guy."

"Right.

"May I ask why?"

"Because I cheated on him with him."

"You mean you cheated on the boyfriend with this other guy."

"Yes."

I got that old queasy feeling of this-can't-be-a-coincidence. Sensing a set-up, I decided to play it safe and save bus/train fare. "Listen, can you just come to my office, say tomorrow afternoon? I am currently without a car, which may preclude me from accepting your case or anyone's for the foreseeable future."

"I can do that. I have a car." It surprised me she was still interested given my mobility handicap. I gave her the address and that was that. I tried not to keep picturing what she looked like based on her voice since I didn't want to set expectations too high. I know how unethical it is to entertain desirous thoughts about a potential client, even back then. Naturally I'd never act on these impulses unless I was certain they were welcome. Or she just wasn't my type. Or I wasn't hers, which was the more likely scenario.

Having nothing else to do between now and then, I went downstairs for some counseling.

"How you holding up, Vic?"

"Still shaking, Doc."

"Yeah, this is a bad piece of luck, my man. But other than being a little tipsy, not like you were speeding. And it wasn't a hit and run. Shit, cops don't even know whether it was intentional. That anonymous tip was your one lucky break."

"I'm thinking they won't be anonymous for long." I told him about the phone call.

"Hm. That's too weird to be a coincidence."

"Well, a baseball player hiring me to find his missing wife who turns out to be my missing girlfriend was too weird to be a coincidence, too." She was the long-lost love, Rose, who I found and then lost again that I told you about.

"Exactly. It wasn't a coincidence. So, listen to your own experience."

"I am. Seeing her tomorrow but keeping my wits about me. I won't volunteer any information beyond what she needs to know. I'll just wait for her to admit she's my witness and best chance of beating this rap. I still won't have a driver's license for a while, but this isn't the first time I'll have a DUI on my record."

"Do me a favor and make sure it's the last?"

I nodded, though I'd promised him that before. My drinking wasn't as bad then as it became soon after, particularly after Doc died. But I'm still here, telling this story to you since you're in no position to judge either, so obviously I cut back at some point. I just wasn't ready back then.

My friend Monica Ivy was performing a burlesque routine in one corner, even though no one was watching her but me. We were fuck buddies and I could tell she wanted more on an emotional level. But ever since I lost Rose again—yes, the ballplayer's wife—the idea of commitment or monogamy had lost all allure to me. After a while sex with Monica seemed to be undermining our friendship, which is what I cherished most. She's living in Portland now with her wife. So, it worked out. Especially for her. At this point it was still messy between us.

Watching her gyrate in her skimpy go-go outfit distracted me from my woes. I went up to her when her number was finished.

"Want to have dinner with me?" I asked.

"I heard what happened, Vic. You need company, I can tell."

Forty-five minutes later we were lying in my upstairs bed and she was full of my fluids.

"I hope you don't wind up in jail, Vic."

"Me too. I don't think the quality of sex would be the same."

She slapped my arm playfully. "I'd miss you."

"I'd miss you too."

"I've been seeing someone."

"I don't need to hear about it."

"Jealous?"

"Only if I know the details."

"I'll spare you."

"Thanks."

"You? Seeing anyone?"

"Please. I was on my way to pick up a hooker when all this shit happened. Serves me right."

"Why didn't you just call me?"

"I don't want to take advantage of our friendship, not more than necessary, anyway. And these lines are getting blurry."

"It's been months since we did this."

"I know. I figured I was overdue for a pity fuck,

especially now."

"Any time, Vic."

"I do love being with you, you know. I just don't know what you see in me."

"You're my hero, you know that."

"I'm nobody's hero. I'm a loser."

"No, you're not. Don't ever say that. You're fundamentally a good person. Despite your many, many, many character flaws. That doesn't change. It's rare to be a good person and that makes you a winner."

"Sweet of you to say, doll. So why do I feel like such a loser? No family, no financial security, no future, so there's three basic reasons. The guy I ran over, Hunter, called me that at the bar when we met. A loser. It's been bugging me ever since, echoing inside my head. Obviously, he hit a nerve."

"Better than hitting your whole body."

"Well, we're definitely not even. Anyway, so he's suddenly gone. I will never be able to wrap my head around the fact a person can just disappear like that. This was the first time it was my fault."

"You don't know that."

"Even if was intentional on his part, I was the unwilling catalyst."

"Unwilling, right."

"I didn't admit to the cops I was fiddling with the radio when it happened."

"What? I didn't know that."

"Nobody does. But me. The fact I'm not being completely honest bothers me too."

"If you were a bad person, it wouldn't bother you at

all."

"You always see the best in me, Monica. You're a great friend."

"And you're my hero."

"No, I'm not."

I got out of bed and paced, feeling restless. "Tomorrow I'm meeting with this woman who called me today. I get the idea she was my mystery witness."

"Why?"

"Hunter told me he got kicked out of Oakland after fucking his friend's gal. She's looking for a missing guy she cheated on her boyfriend with. She lives in Oakland. Her boyfriend is a biker. Might be better if she never finds out I bumped off her lover, though if I take the case, she would. All I'd have to do is to tell her the truth, which I can do even without a car."

"This all sounds like bad news."

"Well, I'm only guessing she's my mystery witness and the babe Hunter was boffing. If he'd never banged his pal's gal he wouldn't have been booted out of his house and wouldn't have wound up sitting next to me in a bar and I would never have come close enough to him to run him over, so maybe it is all his fault. Like if that fucking fish had never climbed out of the sea and grew limbs none of us would be dealing with any of this bullshit. But now that all that has already happened and can't be undone, I hope it is her. Maybe she can help me. Not just with the cops, but to find out who this guy really was."

"Why do you need to know?"

"Because, we have this bond now. Nothing else in common whatsoever, except I was the guy who killed him, accidentally or not."

"You're all agitated. Do you want another blowjob?"

I never turn down two things. The other one is a drink. "Yes, please."

Monica gave the best head of any woman I ever met. I was a fool not to marry her. I was a fool for a lot of reasons. That was the best one, though. One reason I didn't want to hear about her dating other people was I knew she gave them the same head she gave me. Made it, and me by extension, feel a little less special. In fact, one of them was Doc.

Later we went out to a pizza joint called Gaspare's and talked a little more. Mostly we just ate and drank in pregnant silence. I was the one who knocked that up, as usual.

"I guess you and I just weren't meant to be anything more than friends," Monica said rather sadly.

"Nothing is meant to be or not meant to be, Monica. I leaned that after Rose." Up until the recent global pandemic, Rose was the central point between my personal Before and After Times. She was almost as contagious and nearly as deadly as any coronavirus.

Monica knew the score and announced it redundantly like a bored sportscaster. "Because she was the reason you became a private eye to begin with, then a client led you back to her, but it was really her orchestrating the reunion all along, and she wound up disappearing on you again after her husband put you in the hospital."

"Exactly. So, what was the point?"

"You got to see her again for some closure, and you still kept this job."

"I suck at it."

"Yet you've been doing it for so long."

"That's the real mystery."

"We'd have never met if you hadn't moved here to look for her. You'd have never met Doc. Nothing that's happened to you since then would've happened."

"Including this accident."

A tear rolled down her cheek. "Forget it, Vic. Maybe you are a loser. People who can't see their wins might as be losers. Hunter was right."

She got up without finishing her food, even though I reminded her I was her hero. I guess I'd finally convinced her I wasn't.

"You're the better person," I said softly to her, but more to myself, as I sat back down to our pizza.

Monica was not only a better person but deserved better than me. Everybody does. Well, almost everybody. I kept hoping I'd fall in love again one day the way I did with Rose. I wanted to feel like the blissfully naive and idealistic young star-crossed lovers in that Richard Linklater movie *Before Sunset*—a movie that still makes me sob with yearning for my lost youth, but don't tell anybody—that aching, all-consuming, intoxicating desire you felt deep in your soul, that made you both indescribably happy because of its immediacy but inconsolably sad because of its impermanence and ultimate elusiveness. In short, I wanted what I couldn't have. That was part of the attraction to Rose. My heart was addicted to tragedy, and Monica offered too much mundane stability. I still craved the thrill of the damned.

***

The next day all I could do was pace my hardwood office floor waiting for the potential client to show up. I hadn't even asked for her name. I had no phone number for her. She might never come over, and I might never hear from her again. I wasn't thinking clearly due to my trauma and sleep deprivation or else I would've at least asked for her contact info. Then again, she didn't offer it. Maybe she never planned on seeing this through. If she was my mystery witness, maybe she was beginning to hold a grudge against me for running down her lover, even if it was premeditated or at least opportunistic suicide.

But at two p.m. sharp, there was a knock on the door, and I opened it. There she was, wearing a halter top and cut-off jeans and high heels. She was straight out of *Lil' Abner*, like Julie Newmar quality. Statuesque and sensuous, way out of my league, but I was in a league of my own, anyway. Suffice to say, I was immediately smitten. Okay, consumed with lust. In either case, feeling very unprofessional. But long before #MeToo I knew better than to make the first move. For one thing, I was too insecure. Also, too lazy. But I never wanted to put anyone in an awkward position, especially if they were a paying client.

She wore too much makeup, but she was still a natural beauty. Earthy, not glamorous. Her body was curvaceous, and she didn't mind showing it off. She sat down and crossed her gams and I sat across from her trying not to look directly at her cleavage. It's now called "The Male Gaze." I should see an ethical optometrist, I guess.

"First off, what's your name?"

"Raquel."

"Like Welch. Suits you. Raquel what?"

"I'd rather not give you too much info until I know you're the right man for the job, Mr. Valentine."

"Please. I'm barely past forty."

"I'm not even thirty."

"Fair enough, but please, call me Vic."

"A little early to drop the formalities, Mr. Valentine."

"Okay. So, what can you tell me about this missing person?"

"What can you tell me first."

Uh-oh. Was she already showing me her cards? I played mine close anyway. "All I know is you're looking for him and you'd rather your biker boyfriend not know about it."

"You'd rather he didn't even know I was here. He's very jealous."

"Noted. But let's get back to the real reason you're here."

"Real reason?"

"Or fake one. Whatever. What do you need from me, Raquel?"

"I want you to find Hunter."

She might as well have pulled out a hatchet and chucked it at my forehead. "Hunter. Hunter what?"

"Thompson."

"Like the writer?"

"Yes, only he didn't know that, and neither did his folks. Just a coincidence."

"Do you believe in coincidence, Raquel?"

"No."

"Good, neither do I."

"But his family back home is totally illiterate, is my point."

"Back home?"

"Arkansas."

"That where you're from?"

"Me? No. I'm from Texas. Austin."

Figured. For some reason all women I met from Texas were gorgeous and all men ugly (In their defense, I'm just not a dude connoisseur by nature, though Don Johnson looked good in pastels, I will admit). I could never figure it out from a strictly evolutionary standpoint.

"You meet Hunter there?"

"No. My boyfriend grew up with him down there. I met him in Austin."

"Your boyfriend."

"Yes."

"What's his name?"

"Buck."

"Buck what? Owens or Rogers?"

"Very funny. No. What difference does it make?"

"Just want a list of the full cast before we make this movie, Raquel. Right now, my only source of information on this case is you."

"Buck and Hunter were in this white supremacist militia group at one time."

She threw that at me like a hatchet, too. "And?"

"They left it, but it didn't really leave them."

"How about you?"

"What about me? Am I a militant bigot?"

"It would help to know."

"Why?"

"I need to know who I'm dealing with."

"Would that be a deal breaker?"

"It would."

"Then no."

"Not what I need to hear."

"You'll figure it out as you get to know me, if you get to know me. I can't speak for Buck. I know Hunter was trying to make a new life for himself after what happened in Little Rock."

"What happened in Little Rock?"

"Bar fight. He accidentally killed someone. A black man. He was drunk and afraid he might be brought up on hate crime charges in addition to manslaughter."

"So, he left and Buck offered him asylum."

"Offered him a what?"

"Cute."

"How did you know?"

"Just connecting the dots. It's my job." Whew.

"Buck fucks the shit out of me."

"Excuse me?"

"You're wondering why I'm with a drug dealer who was a domestic terrorist and has one hard time. The reason is his large cock."

"I...um...okay." Damn. She was a mind reader too. "Thanks for being so direct. It's a refreshing change, especially in my business."

"That crack on the phone about taking it out in trade could get you sued one day. So don't get any ideas, Mister Vic Valentine. I know you."

"You do?"

"I did my own research before calling you. It was all confirmed within thirty seconds of our initial conversation."

"Oh yeah? Like what do you know about me?"

"You're quite the ladies' man."

"So, my reputation does precede me. Who told you this?"

"I have friends in the burlesque scene."

"You a dancer?"

"Stripper. Nothing fancy. I just take it all off dancing to rock music for drunken perverts."

"I see. Where?"

"Oakland."

"What club?"

"Not telling you yet."

"Look, you already know me a lot more than I know you."

"I went to college. I wanted to be a veterinarian."

"What happened?"

"Too hard."

"I would think so unless you're medically inclined. Not enough to just love animals. Might as well be a professional dog walker."

"Buck sells a lot of heroin and coke, so I don't really have to work. I strip because I love turning men on, especially when they can't have me. It's a power trip, what can I say."

She was mesmerizing. I was in deep trouble. I dove in and kept paddling, unafraid to drown as long as we both stayed wet.

"I'm a part time hooker, too. I've seen you at my place of business."

"That tells me a lot, you know. Because I know where that is."

"I don't work there anymore. I'm no longer in the life. I just like having lots of sex. That's why I slept with Hunter. Well, one reason."

"Hunter. The guy we're looking for."

"The guy I'm looking for, yes."

"Well, let me ask you this. Why do you want to find him?"

"He's suicidal."

My brain screamed *Bingo*! But I kept a poker face. I'm good at that.

"That's why he jumped in front of your car."

Okay, maybe I'm not so good at it. I must've been thinking of checkers.

"I'm not a good person, Vic. But you are. I can tell. That's why I need your help. And you definitely need mine."

I just nodded. She had me right where she wanted me. I belonged to her, body and soul. My soul was worthless, and my body was cheap. Not much of a bargain for her. So, I gave her a discount.

"Well, now we both know where he is, in a grave, so you don't need me," I told her, rather crestfallen at the speed of the inevitable resolution.

"I didn't really want you find him, of course. I know he's dead. Buck and I were at his funeral two days ago."

"So why call me? I mean, I'm the guy that ran him over. Maybe you're setting me up since you hold it against me."

"If that were true, I'd have sent Buck over to beat the shit out of you. Or kill you. I was following Hunter the day he died, and I saw the accident from down the block. He told me he was going to kill himself when Buck kicked him out. That's why I followed him."

"So, what information do you need now?"

"I want to know why he was suicidal."

"Can you tell the cops he was suicidal at least? Now? Officially, sign an affidavit and all that jazz? For my benefit?"

"Only after I confirm."

"Confirm?"

"That he was suicidal."

"Well, he told you he was."

"Yes, but why? He had me. Even if it was only for a few hours. He'd always wanted to fuck me, so I finally let him. He's wanted to since we met, but he was afraid of Buck."

"Hm. Maybe that was his initial way of killing himself. Setting himself up to get knocked off by Buck. Then when Plan A fell through, he resorted to Plan B. Me. Sometimes I come up sooner in the alphabet of choices."

"Buck would never do that. Kill Hunter, that is. Or even hurt him. Not physically, anyway. They are like brothers. Plus, I fuck around on Buck all the time and vice versa. He was my pimp for a while. He likes to watch. In fact, he waited till we finished that night before he pulled Hunter off me. It wasn't just the sex. He had trusted Hunter. He felt betrayed. He should've at least asked permission first, according to Buck."

"But you didn't need Buck's permission."

"Never. Hunter was so depressed, I wanted to give

him a reason to live. I thought I did. Then Buck tossed him out, and I was worried Hunter would actually go through with it."

"And he did."

"Maybe. He was depressed even before he came to Oakland. Something happened. He referred to it several times, but I couldn't get it out of him. If we can find out what it was, I'll be your alibi."

"If not?"

"You're fucked."

"Look, obviously he was despondent because of his run-in with the law, right? Isn't that enough? I bet the cops already got that on him once they pulled his jacket."

"He didn't care about that. He was always in trouble with the cops. I knew him too well. Trust me." Famous last words.

"So, you're still willing to pay my fee and expenses? Even though it's essentially a quid pro quo anyway since my freedom depends on it?"

"I have lots of cash. We're both going to need it. No fee. But all expenses on me."

"Deal."

"Let's go out to my car," she said after she signed a copy of the boiler plate one page (paragraph) contract I kept in my desk. "I have someplace to take you, and something to get out of the way before we get down to business."

By the way, as noted on the contract, her surname wasn't Welch, if that's what you're wondering. It was Fleming, as in Rhonda. Close enough.

Befitting her retro bombshell style, she drove a fire

red 1966 Mustang. Top down. The engine roared like my libido as she peeled out of the parking lot, nearly running over a woman pushing a baby carriage, a guy walking a dog, and an old lady.

"You just have to pay attention," she said as the wind whipped through her thick, dark wavy hair and we sped down Geary toward the Cliff House. "That's the key to everything."

"Thanks for the belated tip."

"Lunch is on me," she said. "But you can leave the tip."

"Business expense?"

"This isn't business yet," she said, putting her hand on my knee as we parked. Then she unzipped my pants and blew me in the passenger seat, right there by Sutro Baths. I didn't try to stop her. Took all of two minutes, but then I had a head start, as it were. She gulped me down like it was an oyster shooter. Definitely a pro. Almost as good as Monica, who wasn't formally trained in this field. She was simply an enthusiast.

Two blowjobs in less than twenty-four hours after a dry spell that made the Sahara look like Niagara Falls. Surely, I was doomed.

"Now I think I know you well enough to proceed."

"You're right. Suddenly I feel like I have a reason to live." I never had a problem with sexually confident or even aggressive women. They don't intimidate me. They turn me on. In fact, I married one. My long-lost love was one. Even my friend Monica fits that bill. I definitely have a type. It's refreshing to me when women (not girls, never been into "girls" even when I was a boy) take charge of their own impulses and turn the tables on the more socially prominent dominant male. Not like I was ever a dominant male. I always preferred being dominated.

Raquel smiled as she licked the rest of my jizz of her lips like a cat cleaning bird blood from its claws, then put on lipstick in the car mirror. She was already my best client ever. I was beginning to think running over Hunter was the worst thing that ever happened to him but the best thing that ever happened to me.

But this sudden act of fellatio wasn't a matter of uncontrollable attraction on her part, trust me. It was strategic. She immediately alleviated the one-sided sexual tension so we could focus on the matter at hand. Monica, on the other hand, wanted to please me, because she was hoping I'd eventually agree to be her boyfriend, even after all these years of friendly fucking. I don't know why I wasn't in love with Monica, though I did love her, and found her extremely appealing physically. I guess she just wasn't dominating enough for my tastes.

"Where are we going after lunch?"

"Los Angeles."

"Why?"

"Because that's where Hunter was before he came to Oakland."

"Why?"

"That's what I need to find out."

"Why do you care why he killed himself?"

"Because I may be pregnant with his child."

Great, I thought. I might've just shot my wad into a Mommy mouth. Not my preferred perversion. I felt ill.

I should've bolted out of that Mustang and ran to the

nearest police precinct and begged them to book me for vehicular manslaughter right then and there. At least I'd be safer in the can than I was in this car.

But like I told Monica, the sex was better on the outside. You can die anywhere, anytime, for no good reason at all. Might as well get what you can while you can.

My recent history just reaffirmed my worst anxieties about sentient existence. Poor Hunter. And all those people you read about in the news dying in car accidents or from disease or poverty or natural disasters. Or suicides or mass shootings or wars. Plus, eventually everyone reading or not reading this right now. It must really suck being dead. For one thing, you'll never know what happens next. Who becomes the next president, what movies are coming out, whatever happens to so-and-so. But that's how it goes in this world and galaxy. Everything can be going along just fine for you personally and then one day you look down and you're pissing blood.

The Hidden

My wife Val, who is sitting with me right now on a park bench in Ravenna Park, near the University of Washington in Seattle, says I'm an unreliable narrator. So does Monica.

For instance, when I called her recently to discuss this

case, which has remained buried in my brain for over two decades, she totally remembered it, though she didn't recall Raquel being quite as hot as I described her. She didn't even remember her name being Raquel. And considering this was a repressed memory for so long, naturally the details that resurfaced after such an extended hiatus are not one hundred percent guaranteed. Not even my wife will vouch for me, and she knows me best. Of course, sometimes I'm not certain she's for real, either.

Full disclosure: I've suffered an increasing number of blackouts and psychotic breaks as I've aged, so naturally this impacts my ability to recall and relate my past to anyone, even myself.

The point is I can't verify the accuracy of every single teeny tiny detail of this story, or any story told from my warped prism. Perhaps I'm embellishing it a tad here and there, particularly regarding anything sexually beneficial to me, but so what? I'm just trying to make it entertaining for you. Much more entertaining that it was for me to experience, and for me to recount. It's more like a confession than a story. You'll see.

Like I said, memories and dreams all get mixed into the same psychic soup as time goes by, and if something wasn't recorded on film for posterity, well, my recall is the best you got. What difference does it make? Dreams defy logic but we accept their rules of engagement anyway, at least while we're in them. That's how I see life.

Problem with this philosophy is the cops will never accept it as a defense.

We were in Half Moon Bay before I realized I wasn't

supposed to be leaving the city limits per the law, not until this matter was resolved, hopefully in my favor.

"But we are resolving it," Raquel said. I couldn't keep my eye off her thigh. Natural instinct.

"Tell them that."

"Okay."

Abruptly she pulled over onto a barren stretch of sand near the foamy beach. The foggy sky and boisterous waves were soul soothing. I would miss them in prison if they booked me on vehicular manslaughter. And I'd definitely miss it one day in the far future six feet underground, though I wouldn't realize it, which makes it even sadder. Suddenly my insides hurt. I didn't want to go to jail. I didn't want to die. I almost cried. It was all so sad and beautiful, like that quote from *Down by Law*.

Raquel reached into the glove compartment and pulled out a Nokia cellphone. I didn't have a cellphone back then, but I knew they existed. Next to the phone was a handgun, a silver semi-automatic.

"What's that for?"

"It's not loaded, just for show and deterrence. Shut up and listen."

She got my precinct on the line and, again remaining anonymous, told them she had kidnapped me in order to prove my innocence. She nodded and then cut them off.

"What did they say?"

"Don't do it."

"And?"

"I just hung up." Then she hit the gas and we peeled out. She was a take-charge kind of gal. Just my type, since I'm basically lazy and stupid. I was almost in love.

"Where exactly in L.A. are we headed?"

"Hollywood. You been there?"

"I know it well. Too well. Bunch of psychos and losers and sex maniacs."

"Then you'll fit right in."

"Why was Hunter there?"

"Staying with a friend."

"Another friend. Biker?"

"No. Stripper."

"Friend of yours?"

"My sister. Rhonda."

"Really. Rhonda Fleming." I told you it was close enough.

"Just a coincidence. I think. My mother did watch a lot of old movies, though."

"Was your father named Ian by any chance?"

"No. Jack."

"Okay."

"He was an asshole."

"For a living?"

"Basically. Never saw him much. My sister and I went to work as teenagers to support our mother."

"Stripping?"

"And hooking. Drugs, whatever."

"Family business?"

"Our mother and grandmother were strippers too. Also prostitutes."

"Hey, I don't judge."

"Who the fuck are you to judge anybody?"

"I'm not! Nobody is. All people suck one way or another."

"Exactly."

"Just not always as literally as you."

She shot me a dirty look and I quickly got back on topic. "So, wait, if he was shacked up with your sister, what's the mystery? Why didn't you just call her?"

"I tried but she won't answer her phone. I asked some mutual acquaintances who haven't seen her either. I'm afraid Hunter might've killed her."

Wow. Another hatchet to the head. Her specialty. "The recently deceased possible father of your potentially unborn child may have killed your sister before allegedly stepping in front of a moving vehicle and killing himself, virtually framing an innocent driver as one last 'fuck you' to the world."

"That's about it."

"Okay. Just wanted to make sure I had it right."

We kept driving down the 101. She was taking the long, scenic route, eschewing the more direct but boring Highway 5 expressway, strange for someone in a hurry. Or maybe she wasn't so anxious to find out the truth or some version of it. I know I was in no rush to be anywhere but here with her.

All the way down she blasted her own mixed tape of classic rock, with songs like "Hush" by Deep Purple, "Roadhouse Blues" by The Doors and "In-A-Gadda-Da-Vida" by Iron Butterfly, making me feel like I was in an early 1970s road movie, when actually it was more like a mismatched buddy road movie plagued with a series of misadventures a la Alexander Payne's Sideways, which hadn't come out yet, so I'm only making that reference in retrospect because I like that movie and I wish it had been that innocuous.

We don't always get to pick the movies we're cast in, though. The reality was Raquel wasn't just some crazy dude I knew from college, like in *Sideways*. I never even went to college. As a traveling companion, she was more my speed anyway—a natural beauty who radiated both sensuality and sadness. Watching her chain smoke and brush back the windswept hair from her sweetly sexy face was both soothing and stimulating. Still, looking back, I'd rather have been with my pal Doc on a mundane odyssey to local wineries on a quest for love. But neither of us drank wine. We often whined about love, though.

Raquel decided to stop for lunch in Monterey. It was still overcast and cool. My kind of climate. It wasn't like this often enough in California, which is one reason I eventually wound up in Seattle.

Raquel was moody and quiet now, and I didn't push any small talk on her. I hate small talk anyway and got the strong idea she did too. The left field revelation about her sister, and the suspicion she was murdered by a dead guy, just added another layer of quicksand into the pit already sucking me under.

Finally, I just had to ask her, "What is this really about? I mean, why do you need me?"

"You have a gun too, right?"

"Yeah, licensed to thrill, baby. Why?"

"You brought it?"

"Of course. Technically, or maybe not, I'm on a case. I only carry it for protection."

"Good. I may need your protection. I think Buck is going to beat us down there."

"Why?"

"He was also fucking my sister."

"Hm."

"Hm what?"

"Did you try calling your sister before or after Buck left town?"

"Before. And again after. He caught me."

"Oh. I thought maybe…"

"He was a suspect in her disappearance?"

"Yeah, it kinda crossed my mind, like a nervous jaywalker."

"Mine, too. But the friends I talked to down there are mutual. I think they may have warned Rhonda that Buck was coming down, so she disappeared herself."

"Okay, so why jump to the conclusion she's dead? Because untimely death is trending in your circles lately?"

"No, she still would've called me and told me where she was hiding."

"Does she know you're on your way down?"

"I have no idea."

"Does Buck?"

"Yes."

"How do you know?"

"I told him."

"Shit, did you tell him about me?"

"No! He knows nothing about you."

"Let's keep it that way."

"Well, at least until we get to L.A."

"Then what?"

"Then we may run into him, I don't know. If we're

both looking for Rhonda, it's bound to happen."

"Why is he looking for Rhonda?"

"Because I think maybe he also blames Hunter's death on her. Though he vowed to kill the person who actually ran Hunter down."

"Wait, what?"

"That's what got me thinking the same thing."

"No, I mean—he's looking for me?"

"Well, he's looking for the unidentified motorist responsible for Hunter's death. But even he suspects it was suicide. He plans to beat the motorist until he gets more details, since the police won't offer us any information until their investigation is over."

"Okay, hold it. You're talking about this 'unidentified motorist' in the third person, when he's sitting right in front of you."

"Your name wasn't mentioned in the newspaper. Even Hunter's obituary said the identity of the motorist was being concealed until it could be determined it was manslaughter."

"Of course, you know that motorist's identity."

"Only because I happened to be there when it happened."

"Wouldn't it be easier for everyone, especially me, if you just released your own identity to the cops and cleared me?"

"I only saw you run him over. I can't say whether it was an accident or not."

"Well, did he run or jump in front of the car?"

"He just kept walking, like he didn't see you, but it was impossible for him not to see you at such close range.

Plus, you weren't going very fast."

"There you go! That's all the cops need to know."

"It's not all I need to know."

"So, this is all about you now."

"I'm offering to give the cops an alibi for you once I can back it up with facts. That's why we're going to L.A."

"Where the guy who wants to kill me is headed too."

"Buck was the one who gave me the idea it was suicide. Or maybe I brought it up and gave him the idea. I don't remember. Forgive me, I'm a bit stressed lately."

"I understand. So why not go with Buck and find out together?"

"Because I'd rather go with you. I don't trust him."

"Why?"

"Did I tell you he's fucking my sister?"

"Oh. Does he know you know?"

"It's been behind my back. That's why I don't trust him. We had a fight over Hunter, so I confronted him about Rhonda since he was being a total hypocrite. He could've just told me a long time ago."

"Why didn't he, you think?"

"They're hiding something besides an affair."

"About Hunter."

"See? You are a good detective."

"Just a lucky guesser. Anyway, are you really being straight with me right now?"

"I'm trying to." Then she broke down and started crying. Now I was totally invested in this case, regardless of the outcome, not just for my sake, but for hers. My heart softened even while my dick hardened.

That's when I knew this couldn't end well, but it was

too late now. I was already being taken for a long ride.

Hollywood

Hollywood is a minefield of fragile egos. I've had to sidestep them several times during both professional and personal sojourns down to the sunny Southland. But everyone sees those daily entertainment headlines about some spoiled celebrity whining because a critic or co-star said something they interpreted as undermining their prestige and potential in the industry, which results in lawsuits or a war of words or tabloid fodder. The desperation in the air is thicker than smog. But the gals were gorgeous and the Googie-style coffee shops were ginchy. It was fun to visit, though I had no desire to live or die there.

During our road trip Raquel and I discussed matters of love, sex, movies, music, life, and death. She was really quite smart and worldly, despite what society's snobs may consider to be her low-brow lifestyle choices. She was very well read and had an interesting take on just about any topic I broached. Mostly I wanted to know more about the guy I killed, but that was the one subject that wasn't open to discussion.

She seemed to relax by the time we crossed the Grapevine. I tend to grow on people quickly once they get past my defense mechanisms, like contagious fungus. We had a natural rapport that I hoped might translate into more carnal knowledge down the road, but for now we were partners on a case, and I still wasn't sure whether it was a murder mystery or just a psychological noir. As long as it had elements of an erotic thriller either or neither was fine with me.

Speaking of which, her favorite movie was the 1984 Brian De Palma flick *Body Double*. It had always made her want to live in L.A., she told me. In fact, her second favorite movie was William Friedkin's 1985 flick *To Live and Die in L.A.* I liked those a lot, but I told her my favorite L.A. movie was *Repo Man*. "Plate of shrimp," she said. Man, I really liked her.

"So why don't you live here instead of Oakland?"

"I used to, with Rhonda and Buck, when we all left Austin a few years ago. But then Buck was invited to join the Oakland chapter of Hell's Angels, and we moved up there. By then my sister was getting heavy into Satanism, so it was just as well. It was getting weird and creepy being around her."

"What? Your sister is a devil worshipper?"

"Yup. She got into it when we lived briefly in New Orleans, but then in L.A. she hooked up with some witches and eventually joined their coven. Blood rituals, voodoo ceremonies in the woods, orgies, all that. Just like those old drive-in movies."

"Wow. I hope I get to meet her." Technically voodoo and Satanism are two totally different religions, but I let it pass. Maybe her sister was covering all her bases.

Needless to say, unlike the late Hunter, Raquel was not religious or patriotic. She was never a white supremacist, either. She was just testing my boundaries.

"I've had more black dick than Pam Grier," she told me. I found that hard to believe, but the pictures that statement put in my mind gave her the benefit of the doubt.

And as stated, we also talked about stuff like life and death.

"What do you think happens when we die?" she asked me, like I would know.

"My worthless opinion? Nothing. We cease to exist."

"So, you don't think there's a greater intelligence at work in the universe?"

"Maybe, maybe not. Regardless, we as individual semi-sentient sacks of shit are finite. Our body and mind stop functioning, we're gone for good."

"So, consciousness of existence just ends."

"Because we no longer exist, right."

"That's depressing."

"I agree. I try not to think about it."

She was very quiet after that, maybe thinking about Hunter. Me, I was just thinking about myself, as usual.

It was twilight when we rolled into the City of Angels, or City of Angles as I liked to say, which was a perfect time of day to appreciate the sprawling neon splendor of L.A. I started singing the theme to *77 Sunset Strip* and snapping my fingers, and Raquel joined in. Our first stop per my request was at Norm's on Pico. It was one of the few Googie-style shops still standing in L.A. Ships in Westwood, my favorite, was long gone, and the original Ben Frank's on Sunset was now a Mel's Diner. A consciously retro, commercially nostalgic chain just ain't the same. Rae's in Santa Monica was still around, but this

Norm's was closer to Hollywood. Also, this was long before I went full vegan, so I could actually order a scrambled egg breakfast for dinner.

She'd called ahead and booked us a room at one of my favorite places to stay in L.A., the ultra-retro Beverly Laurel Hotel on Beverly Boulevard, not far from one of my favorite local spots, the Farmer's Market, per my suggestion. The vintage 1960s vibe suited my tastes more than hers, but that was okay. She was here for business, which is why she booked a room with twin beds. "We can always push them together later," I told her after we dropped off our belongings. She rolled her eyes which was not the response I was going for, but I was patient, especially since she'd already crossed that line without any encouragement from me.

She always kept some extra stuff in the trunk of her Mustang. On the way out the door I'd tossed some socks and underwear into a sack at her suggestion, since she warned we'd be gone a few days. I would be wearing my trademark rumpled Tokyo Drifter/Rat Pack sharkskin suit, white shirt, and skinny black tie for the duration. Except when I was in bed, of course.

Which is why it was so unfortunate I got blood on it, my blood, as soon as we walked out the door and onto the outer street, on the way to hit some strip clubs in search of her missing sister. I noticed the big hog parked rather haphazardly nearby before a fist hit me full force in the face and I spurted red gunk onto my white shirt. Fortunately, it missed the suit and tie. Yes, these were the first thoughts on my mind, at least before the second punch, right in my gut, made me double over in agony with tears bursting spontaneously from my blurry eyes. I heard Raquel screaming expletives and then in my peripheral vision vaguely perceived a scuffle between her and my assailant. I already knew who it was.

"Buck, stop it!" she insisted as she slapped her biker boyfriend around the head. He grabbed her by her wrists and pushed her down before kicking me in the shin, and then kicking me more in the face and stomach when I was down on the sidewalk. It seemed to me that any passing pedestrians were crossing the street to avoid the situation.

I passed out briefly but regained semi-consciousness quickly. While lying there all dopey and bloody with no one offering assistance or empathy, I picked up on bits and pieces of conversation between Raquel and Buck, who had finally calmed down enough to engage in relatively civilized discourse. I guess he'd momentarily finished flushing some violent impulses out of his system at my expense.

Naturally I don't recall exact dialogue but the gist of it was Buck had already found Rhonda and was willing to take us to her, or rather just Raquel. But then Raquel said I was on her payroll as a bodyguard, which elicited loud laughter from Buck. That's when I pulled out my .38 from my back waistband, wobbled to my feet, and pointed it right at his stupid face. He was big, beefy, bearded, and ruggedly handsome in that macho redneck kind of way.

Raquel stepped up and told me nicely to put it away. I lowered it and then Buck swung and knocked me down again, sending my gun flying across the sidewalk. After that I felt someone, probably Buck, picking me up and tossing me into the backseat of the Mustang, then felt the cool night air on my fucked-up face as the car sped somewhere, hopefully a hospital.

No such luck. We wound up at a nightclub somewhere in Hollywood called Satanic Rites. Rhonda parked in the back lot and Buck rolled up next to us. She smacked my already bruised cheeks to rouse me back to life, even though it hurt like hell, which I guess was the point. Then she told me she once danced here and knew it well. Turned out it was a front for an actual Satanic cult that owned the property, though there were real strippers with real boobs dancing on the back stage as we walked in.

The interior was lined with plush old-school booths and the lighting glowed red like they were developing dirty photographs. The walls were all wood-paneled and sported velvet nude paintings and blown-up photographs of girlie mag centerfolds from the '60s and '70s. The long bamboo bar lining one side of the oblong room was stocked with good whiskey, rum, and gin, so it wasn't a dive.

This place was gaudy but well-financed. The music was a mix of Bauhaus, The Cramps and Sisters of Mercy, suiting the goth-punk vibe. Customers were dressed—many barely dressed—almost exclusively in leather, and I already knew from all the bikes out front that many of Buck's pals hung out here. The two sizzling-hot strippers on stage recognized Raquel and Buck, I could tell, though they only nodded acknowledgement of our presence. Well, Buck and Raquel. I was simply ignored, but I'm used to that.

At least it was dark enough that my bloody shirt didn't really register as we all squeezed into a booth and Buck ordered a round of beers and shots from the topless waitress. I noticed there were four TVs mounted on the walls, one in each corner. One was playing *The Devil's Wedding Night* from 1973, another *The Devil's Rain* from 1975, another *Race with the Devil*, also from '75, and the last was showing *Satan's Slave* from 1976.

Only someone like me would recognize all four instantly, and I was both enthralled and impressed with the curator's choices, especially since at the time at least two of them must've been bootlegs. Not even Doc had them on tape yet. The movies played without sound, just like at The Drive-Inn, which seemed so far away now. I'd seen them all on 42nd Street back in New York, when grindhouse cinema ruled my world. Those sleazy movies still ruled my world, except now I was living in one, which wasn't quite as comfortable.

"Oh, poor baby, are you okay?" Raquel finally asked as she gently touched my wounds. I winced and she withdrew her gesture. I was sitting between them, feeling claustrophobic and paranoid. But when we sat down, my gun, which had been tucked into the side of Buck's jeans after he apparently retrieved it from the street, fell out next to me onto the booth. I managed to quickly repossess it, hiding it beneath my leg.

"Fuckin' pussy," Buck said in my humble regard without even looking at me, downing his shot then chasing it with the beer in a single gulp, signaling the waitress for another. The way they looked at each other I could tell they got it on at some point. I noticed Raquel noticed too, but she decided to remain focused on the mission.

"So, where the fuck is Rhonda?" she demanded.

"Probably in back, getting ready. She's on the bill tonight, trust me."

"Did Mephisto tell you that?"

"Yes. Relax."

"Mephisto, like the Devil?" I asked.

"Shut the fuck up," Buck said, so I did, for now.

"Leave him alone," Raquel said, just touching my shoulder this time. "I'm sorry I got you into this, Vic."

"Not like I can just leave now. You're my ride."

"I warned you."

"After we were already on the road."

"I said shut the fuck up!" Buck reminded me. "And yeah. Mephisto is The Devil. So, unless you want your soul sacrificed, I'd play invisible 'til further fuckin' notice."

"Seriously?"

Buck elbowed me in the jaw and I spit blood from my split tongue. Raquel slapped Buck on the back of his head, but he didn't even flinch.

"You fuck this loser too?"

"No, she just blew me," I said with a lisp.

Enraged, Buck raised his fist in clobbering mode, but I was ready with my gun, which I stuck between his big, surprised eyes.

"Put that away now," a deep voice demanded calmly from the nearby shadows.

Complying with the request, I looked up and saw a tall, indeterminately ethnic man sporting a Fu Manchu mustache, slick black hair pulled back into a ponytail from a severe widow's peak, a smoothly bare muscular chest, tight leather pants, shiny black boots, and a long red cape. He was standing patiently next to our table like he was about to take our order. But somehow I doubted he had a subservient station in life, at least not in this joint, which I instinctively knew belonged to him. He had long claw-like fingernails and piercing black eyes. Yup, he was Satan all right. Maybe not the one and only, more likely just an early example of overzealous geeky fan boy cosplay. I proceeded with caution just the same, operating under the safest assumption given my circumstances.

"Vic, meet Mephisto," Raquel said. "Real name Martin—"

The devil dude rudely interrupted the polite introduction by instantly jerking Raquel's head back by her hair. Then he leaned over, licked her tense face, reached down into her cleavage and fondled her left breast, and finally let go with a sinister smile. Of course, this was way before Harvey Weinstein got busted and this kind of behavior became widely frowned upon by the general public. At the time no one voiced objection to this degradation, not even me, but I was biding my time for the most opportune moment to intervene. Buck looked away nervously, avoiding eye contact. How gallant. I just kept my hand on my gun beneath the table.

It struck me that while I had thought I was getting mixed up with Neo-Nazis, which would've been bad enough, instead I found myself smack in the midst of a Satanic sex cult, with a leader who took his role so literally it was comic-bookish.

Marty Mephisto, as I now called him mentally, since he cut off Raquel before she revealed his surname, eyeballed me with ice cold consideration, making me shiver in a frigid fever that came on suddenly. This optical equivalent to a game of hot rod chicken seemed to last a long time, but it was probably only a moment or less. Still, I felt like I was slowly coming out of a coma. Finally, Marty declared victory in the staring contest and when I looked down and my vision refocused, I noticed the swastika tattooed on Buck's right hand. So Neo-Nazis too, on top of Satanists. Maybe I would've been better off back in a San Francisco jail awaiting arraignment on vehicular manslaughter charges. Too late now. All my options were lousy.

"She'll be right out," Marty said before he abruptly walked away. I figured he meant Rhonda, correctly, since the spotlight hit the stage not far from our table and there was a gyrating gal with more than a passing resemblance to Raquel already pulling her sparkling G-string off, leaving on nothing but her pumps and perspiration.

"Why didn't she answer your calls, you think?" I asked Raquel.

"Why are you still talking?" Buck said, glaring at me, though with less credible intimidation than before. Marty Mephisto had marked this turf as the dominant alpha male.

I stuck the business end of the .38 in his thigh and kept talking.

"Raquel, please, just answer me. What the hell is this? Why are we even here?"

"I think Rhonda got Hunter mixed up in this thing, against his will, by casting a spell on him."

"Really? Like Screamin' Jay Hawkins?"

"That's a black man," Buck said. "She ain't no—"

"Hey nobody's talking to you, David Duke," I said, pressing the gun deeper into Buck's leg. It pushed back reflexively. The guy was built like a leather-bound tank.

Rhonda was watching her sister dance as if in a trance, but she said to me, "Vic, I'm going to take you to the airport. You should just go home."

"To what? I need your eyewitness testimony to make sure I stay out of the cooler."

The topless waitress who looked like a refugee from one of Russ Meyer's wettest dreams brought another round of drinks, on the house, courtesy of "Mister M." The dark mystery booze was poured over ice in tumblers. Whatever it was tasted good.

Then after a few more I blacked out. Not sure how long I was out, but it felt like days. I dreamed about a cat I once saw alone in a field at night while I was driving around in Oakland. The lonely image haunted me ever since. I'd always wondered what happened to him, or her, and wished I'd stopped the car and rescued him/her. In the dream I wasn't in my Corvair. I was walking home from school, because your subconscious always mixes up memories into a surrealistic soup. I went out to the field and brought the cat, who kept changing colors, home to my house in Brooklyn where I grew up. My mother, who died in an insane asylum, was there, along with my brother, who committed suicide by jumping off a local bridge. Of course, in my dreams they were forever alive and well. Well, maybe not so well. Maybe not so alive, either. The cat seemed to make them happy. But then the cat starting yowling and vomiting like it was possessed by the Devil. I looked over at my mother and brother, who were both levitating in the air, eyes rolled back in their heads as they violently convulsed and drooled gore. Then the three zombies just burst into dust and disappeared. I was suddenly all alone in the dark house. My father wasn't home because he was never home.

The loneliness made my soul ache. It was the loneliness that had plagued me for most of my life and often made me want to die. My dreams were always as vivid as my waking life, and sometimes more so, to the point where I had trouble distinguishing the two.

I suddenly found myself in the middle of an orgy, not sure if this was still part of the same dream or just a whiplash segue. I hoped I was still dreaming. In any case, I just rolled with it, since even in the depths of depression I could rub one out to release tension. Sex dreams were always preferable to death dreams, but your dreams choose you, not vice versa. This was a definite improvement.

I scanned my surroundings, searching for a clue regarding the veracity of the situation. If I was still dreaming, and realized it, I could fuck anyone with impunity, like one of my adolescent wet dreams. If it wasn't, there could be trouble, because once you start mingling genitals with strangers, anything could happen, probably something bad. This was why I preferred dreams to real life. For the freedom. The fun kind.

The windowless room was professionally lit like a

soundstage, and indeed 35mm cameras were rolling from two different vantage points. The walls were lined with crimson drapes and the floor was covered with shag carpeting of the same hue. There were beautiful bodies of both sexes in various stages of hardcore fornication surrounding us, and in the middle of the room was our pal Marty Mephisto, ominously holding a long, gleaming silver dagger with a jewel encrusted handle over a heavily sedated, nubile young woman lying naked on an altar, unshackled and seemingly unperturbed by her predicament.

A giant pentagram was being projected onto one of the curtains. Another very tall, imposing person, probably male, was standing in the corner, overseeing the pulpy proceedings, wearing a black gown and a big fake goat head with massive horns. At least I hoped it was fake, though it sure looked real. Obviously, I was hallucinating, I thought. Then I noticed Buck and Raquel were among the assembled lovers, whereas I was tied to a chair. My hands were bound, so I couldn't even jerk off.

As my vision resumed full clarity, I noticed the young woman about to get stabbed in the name of Satan, or so I presumed, was Rhonda. Then as my senses recovered full function, if only within a fever dream context, I realized I was also stark-raving naked. The whole thing was like a scene from an old Paul Naschy movie or my personal favorite, *Satan's Blood* (1977).

Two hippie-looking goons untied me from the chair and then lifted my body to the altar, placing me on top of ravishing Rhonda, who embraced me, wrapping her long legs around my barrel-shaped torso and forcing me into her without much effort. I was already erect from witnessing the orgy, so the erotic encounter was over and done in about three deliriously decadent minutes. That's all the time any of us needed, since Rhonda and I shared rapturous release simultaneously while our witnesses watched and wanked.

After I had finished unloading my corporeal essence into her writhing sister, I looked over and saw Raquel was standing beside us, sobbing. "How could you, Vic?"

"Sorry, baby," I said insincerely. "The Devil made me do it."

Then I felt Marty Mephisto's long silver dagger plunge into my back, through my chest, and into Rhonda's heart. I didn't feel pain, though. More like an intense pressure, as if psychosomatic. Our bodily fluids merged and dripped over the side of the table onto fellow revelers reposed in post-coital bliss. But it hadn't been ol' Marty Mephisto who shish-kabobed us. It was Raquel, standing there with our blood dripping from the blade onto her bare heaving breasts.

"Cut!" Marty Mephisto said. "That's a wrap!"

A strange, glowing blue mist swirled through the room like a disco fog machine, engulfing and obscuring all, at least from my viewpoint, which subsequently faded to black.

Hypnosis and Hallucinations

I woke up alone in a cold sweat and warm bed. Groggy but resolute, I pulled myself up onto my feet. My sharkskin suit, bloody white shirt, skinny tie, boxer shorts, socks and shoes were laid out for me. No sign of my gun, of course. I'd lost those privileges. The gloomy little room, more like a cell with a tiny window, was barren except for the bed and a sink, which I used to splash my face after I'd dressed. Then I pissed in it. I used to do that often when I lived in residential hotels with communal restrooms.

My urine ran red down the drain. I chalked it up to internal damage incurred during my recent rough treatment. But as a chronic hypochondriac, I can't say I wasn't nervous. Of course, getting beaten up was a long-standing job hazard. I got beat up a lot as a kid in Brooklyn too. The only difference now was I got paid for it.

I checked the door, and it was predictably locked. I got on my tippy-toes to peer out the window, but I was in a basement so I didn't see much besides grass and sunlight. At least that told me it was daytime. What day was a wild guess.

"You're awake at last," a voice said from beyond like a Bond villain. I looked around and noticed a tiny monitor in one corner of the ceiling.

Then the door opened. It was Raquel, dressed in a see-through silk gown and high-heeled slippers. For a second, I hoped I was a prisoner in the bowels of Playboy Mansion.

Oddly and thankfully, she didn't seem mad at me anymore. She gave me a kiss then sat me down on the bed, stroking my forehead, which was still sore from all the violent action.

"Back from the dead, I see," she said. "So, my sister's spells do work."

"What? I'm a zombie? I mean in the Val Lewton sense, not George Romero."

"I don't get the first reference, but not exactly, Vic. See, Hunter thought Rhonda's black magic made him immortal, so he put it to the test."

"Fail."

"Yes. But now we know it can work."

"I didn't notice any stab wounds when I was getting dressed."

"Well, not everything is what it seems, Vic."

"I get the idea I might still be under a spell." Sinatra sang "Witchcraft" in my head, but he often does that.

"That's possible."

"So, this could all be an illusion, induced by hypnosis or narcotics?"

"Perhaps."

"You don't know."

"No one knows anything, Vic."

"No shit. Thanks for the crash course in my field of expertise. So, you found your sister and you admit Hunter tried to kill himself because he thought he'd get up and walk away."

"Yes."

"So, are we done?"

"I am. You're not."

"Why the hell not?"

"Because I brought you here as a test subject, Vic.

That's what this is all about."

"Why me?"

"Because you ran over Hunter. This is the price."

"Can't I just go to jail like a normal drunk driver?"

"Well, you're being held captive. Close enough?"

"No. Where are we, exactly?"

"The basement of the club. Beneath the private theater."

"Where the orgy took place."

"Orgy? What orgy?"

"Okay, so it's like that. That was the drug-induced 'dream sequence' part of the plot. Got it. So, you're telling me you're in this cult?"

"It's not a cult. It's a private path to ultimate enlightenment. But it will be open to the public once refined."

"That's a yes. Was anything you told me true?"

"Some of it, sure."

"Why did Buck beat me up?"

"To subdue and manipulate you with violent misdirection, feeding into the stereotype I planted in your mind."

"To get me where you wanted me, you mean."

"Yes. Also, he just doesn't like you."

"I see. He hasn't really given me much of a chance, but since I don't like most people, chances are I wouldn't like him either, so it's mutual. Good to know who's who and what's what at least, if belatedly. Is Hunter still dead at least?"

"Of course."

"Was I really dead?"

"Just drugged. But we're testing the limits of your physical and psychic senses after being exposed to our potions."

"Jesus. Buck is in this thing too?"

"Yes. He was the one who introduced me to Martin."

"Mephisto."

"That's his stage name and public persona. He's also an actor."

"I'll bet. I saw the cameras. I guess I am now, too."

"An actor? More or less. More like the subject of a documentary."

"A documentary? So, this will be shown in film festivals? I'll be famous?"

"More like it's, shall we say, an industrial film for our investors."

"Your accent. It's gone."

"What accent?"

"Exactly."

"Oh. I'm really from here. San Fernando Valley. So is Buck. His real name is Dave."

"And you?"

"I used to be Sherry, but Raquel is my real name now. Well, one of them. For now."

"Whatever. So, Buck or Dave or whoever, he's not actually a bigoted biker, you're not a stripper who turns tricks. All of this is smoke and mirrors for my benefit?"

"Not yours exclusively. The outside world's. The media's. Law enforcement. We just pose as right-wing religious Confederate Southerners so people will keep their distance, especially here on the Left Coast."

"So, this set-up isn't political in nature."

"Everything is political, Vic. But this is more spiritual."

"In a fucked up kinda way maybe."

"Sometimes you need darkness to see the light."

"Nice bumper sticker. When can I go?"

"You sure you want to?" She let a strap fall off her shoulder. Since her gown was see-through, nothing was left to the imagination anyway.

"You offering me sex again?"

"Again?"

"Well, the blowjob, which I see now was a way to instantly put me under your spell. As it were."

"I don't consider fellatio to be sex, but since you see it that way, that I was trying to seduce and control you, did it work?"

"Yeah, but I'm easy, so I wouldn't put much stake in my reactions to any of this jazz. I'm a lousy test subject. Ask anybody."

"This is all part of the plan, Vic."

"Plan? You knew I'd run Hunter over, even by accident?"

"There are no accidents, Vic."

"So, on purpose then. How could you know what I was going to do in advance?"

"I didn't. But it happened and a plan revealed itself. That's how we know it was meant to be. Deliberate action is often a direct response to unforeseen events. Whatever sets a series of circumstance in motion is called a catalyst."

"Gee, didn't know that, thanks. I'm glad you finally dropped the white trash bimbo act."

"I had a couple of years at UCLA before I dropped out

to help the cause and pursue my real calling in life."

"What was your major?"

"Double major in Drama and Psychology. I'm an actress, too."

"Psychology? You must've minored in Irony. The acting part, that's obvious now. You're good, kid. Real good. I bought everything, and I'm no sucker. Except for a pretty face, but you knew that, so it was all factored into the trap. Bottom line is you're not really a Satanist, either."

"That's just another front, another layer of protection from the outside world."

"So, what the fuck are you about then?"

"We want to solve the mystery of life and death through magic and sex. Because sex begets life, life is magic, and death is a mystery. See how it all ties together?"

"Not really."

"You're still out of it from the potions in your alcohol."

"So, this is actual witchcraft."

"That's a quaint term, but if that helps you, fine."

"Then what?"

"Call it whatever you like, Vic. Everything around us is ephemeral, merely an illusion. We're just trying to understand its purpose."

"Who isn't? Hardly original. Sorry, that's my existential angst being obstinate."

"Traditional religions are too concerned with dogma. This cuts through the crap."

"Really?"

"Really."

"No one will ever believe this."

"Exactly. We don't want to face exposure until we're ready to reveal the ultimate truth."

"Which is?"

"If I knew that we'd be exposed already, silly."

"What if I tell all this to the cops?"

"Try it."

"Aw, shit. You're right. No one will ever believe this. And you'd hide the proof anyway. Probably already have."

"For many years now. But we don't take chances either. That's why you've been programmed to forget it once you leave here."

"Drugs?"

"Hypnosis."

"Am I hypnotized right now?"

All of a sudden, she looked like a female vampire from a Jean Rollin flick, but maybe that was just me. "Look into my eyes, Vic…" Then she leaned in and kissed me, and we made love or had sex or whatever you want to call it. I guess she forgave me for fucking her sister. If I even fucked her sister. If she even had a sister. If any of this I'm telling you ever even happened.

This is the conundrum of an unreliable narrator. I know because unreliable narrators were my only witnesses to this case.

Raquel was also my sole link to Hunter's life before his death under the wheels of my Corvair. I was obsessed with trying to figure out who he was, if only retroactively via secondhand anecdotes. I grilled her after I drilled her in bed:

58

"Was Hunter a good guy or a bad guy?"

"Nobody can be distilled that simply, Vic."

"Basically, though. He was one or the other."

"He was a good guy who let himself get corrupted. I tried to help him, by showing him a different path. He rejected it. He retreated to his childhood cocoon of religion and patriotism."

"Was he really from Alabama?"

"Arkansas."

"Whatever."

"Yes. I met him when I was in Austin. Dave was with me."

"So, Dave wasn't a childhood friend of Hunter's?"

"No, but they became good friends. Hunter was in a band we saw there all the time. We all three hung out. Dave and I were doing local theater. I'd just left New Orleans where I was staying with my sister. She was the one into Satanism and voodoo."

"So that part was real."

"Yes."

"What does that have to do with this?"

"Martin was my acting coach in Austin. I told him about my sister, and he found it fascinating. He opened this club shortly after we returned to L.A. He knows a lot of rich people who invested in the enterprise. Some of them are actually Satanists. Or hedonists, as they prefer. Pagans, you know."

"Hippies."

"Sure, okay, since you seem to put everyone in prefab categories. But Martin just wanted to expand the borders of consciousness. Dave and I were down for it. Then Dave scored a regular gig with Berkeley Rep and moved to Oakland."

"Not Hell's Angels."

"No, but he does have a motorcycle."

"He sure dresses the part."

"He's a Method actor."

"And all the world's a stage and we're merely the players and all that jazz."

"Exactly."

"Taking it kinda literally, no?"

"The Bard said it, not me, or you."

"Whatever. Did Hunter go with you or stay in Austin?"

"He went back home, then got into that bar fight."

"Where he killed a black man."

"Yes. He'd been radicalized by some white supremacists as a youth, so this came back to haunt him because of some stuff on his record. Dave offered him refuge. Then I fucked Hunter and it got complicated. I was in love with Hunter. That's what bothers Dave the most."

"Dave is in love with you then."

"Dave is, yes."

"I still feel like I don't know who Hunter is or was. I never will, I guess."

"None of us did. But he was actually our friend. Why do you care so much?"

"Because I killed him, even by accident. It haunts the shit out of me."

"Knowing him won't change that. Might just make it worse."

"Maybe you're right. He just seemed like a lost soul."

"He was."

"So did he throw himself in front of my car or not?"

"Yes."

"You saw it."

"Yes.

"You'll tell the cops that."

"Yes. If you follow through."

"On what?"

"You're still on a case, remember. In fact, you are the case. My cash is still on the table."

"For what? Not as a bodyguard, obviously. Certainly not as a detective."

"As a test subject. I promised Martin I'd bring him somebody, and that's you."

"So, you're experimenting on me with mind-altering drugs?"

"Yes, amongst other things."

"Well, that's royally fucked up."

"Actually, not drugs. I lied about that."

"Just that?"

"You were hypnotized."

"Starting when?"

"Back upstairs. By Martin."

"You're kidding. That why I passed out and dreamed I was fucking your sister on a sacrificial altar?"

"Well, some of that actually happened, but your perception of it is skewed."

"Which part was real?"

"You fucked my sister."

"You okay with that?"

"Yes. I'm not in love with you."

"Good for you. Is she? I mean okay with fucking me."

"I doubt she remembers it."

"So just another date for me. Did Hunter fuck your sister?"

"Yes. But it was worse. He fell in love with her."

"Meaning he chose voodoo over whatever this thing is."

"Yes. I thought I could lure Hunter back by pretending I shared my sister's beliefs."

"Why is she here and not in New Orleans?"

"Martin paid her to be in his films."

"What films?"

"The porn films."

"Shit! So that orgy was real?"

"No, it was staged."

"But people were actually fucking."

"Yes.

"Even me."

"Even you."

"Against my will."

"Martin wants to know what you remember, and how you remember it."

"Why?"

"I told you. He's trying to figure out how much of reality is determined by our consciousness of it. His theory is that life is like a dream where if you wake up before it's too late, you can control it."

"Not sure where I fit in."

"His hypnosis techniques are new but revolutionary, especially since he can influence another's mind via the power of simple, sustained eye contact."

"So, there was nothing in my drink?"

"Yes. Whiskey."

"Sometimes that's enough to make me see things. I want to talk to this Marty Mephisto."

"He wants to talk to you. Now. Upstairs. Everyone is waiting. Dinner is being served."

"Good."

"Just one thing. Don't call him Marty Mephisto."

"He's the one calling himself Mephisto. I just added his real name."

"But he was in character then. Now he's just Martin, the spiritual seeker, and teacher."

"The fucking nutcase if you ask me."

"I didn't."

My stomach growled like a cornered panther. "Let's go."

Even though we smelled like fresh, nasty sex and Raquel was dressed more for the boudoir than the dining room, she led me out the door and down a spiral staircase, through an underground tunnel. Which was kind of cool, reminding me of another one beneath the Cal-Neva Resort in Tahoe, Sinatra's old joint. We arrived at the main floor of the mansion, which was located behind the strip club. I hadn't noticed it when we first pulled up, given my battered state of semi-consciousness, but both were on the same property.

The mansion, tucked into the hillside like a fallen beehive, was basically *Psycho* meets *The Addams Family* with a touch of *Scooby Doo* as envisioned by Rob Zombie. An adjacent structure to the strip club, it was located just past the parking lot, and indeed it had a backlot feel. I only finally saw the exterior when I was fleeing from it, but that comes a little later, hang in there.

We were seated at the oblong dinner table in the ostentatiously decorated dining room, which immediately made me think of the Haunted Mansion at Disneyland, maybe intentionally even though that kitschy reference seriously undermined the fear factor, if any was intended. There was an elegant element of Hammer's *Dracula* films, but that perhaps was too generous. It was more like the dinner scene in *The Texas Chainsaw Massacre* if Leatherface won the hillbilly lottery. These clowns were getting harder to take seriously. I relaxed and even drank one of the cocktails served by the Russ Meyer Waitress. Not out of trust, just apathy.

Marty Mephisto was now dressed in a tux, more Bela Lugosi than Christopher Lee, while Raquel remained in her slinky Ingrid Pitt as Marcilla/Carmilla Karnstein semi-attire, which was fine with everyone. The cast included Biker Buck AKA Dave AKA Who Gives a Fuck; Rhonda who was dressed in a tight, form-fitting leopard print jumpsuit and high heels—meow I can't believe I got to hit that; the two hippie henchmen who escorted me to the altar, still dressed like hippie henchmen; and just some random cultists who stared at Marty in dumb admiration, and I do mean dumb.

I just didn't understand the appeal of cults, unless it's a cult movie. But like I told Hunter before I ran him over, I don't do tribes. I'm a lone wolf by nature. Never been sure exactly what that means but it sure sounds hip.

Chicken, fish, and some kind of beef situation were

the main dishes. As I said, at that point I was far from being a vegan like I am now, thanks to my wife, but I never ate red meat, even then, so I went with the fish. And since I wanted to be a polite guest, I did what you're supposed to do when sharing a meal: talk about your day.

"So, are you guys really Satanists, or is this just a cult of fucking actors?" I said, breaking the ice, not that any thawing was truly required. We'd already been pretty intimate, as I recalled.

They all chuckled in a condescending way, then Marty said, "What better way to practice our craft than to concoct narratives with real people in real situations in real time?"

"Scratch that," I said. "You're just a gang of self-centered lying assholes. You should go into politics."

"We're more like an improv group," Raquel said. "With a higher purpose."

"Do you ever take five? I mean, at what point do you just calm down and live your life like normal people? Or even abnormal ones? Can you really live in a perpetual state of make believe?"

"It's Halloween every day in this house," Marty said, sipping his wine.

"You're all delusional. I don't believe you even make porn films."

"You'll believe it after dinner," Dave said.

"Yes, dinner and a movie," Marty said. "It's a date."

"I'm sorry for calling you Marty Mephisto," I said with fake sincerity.

'Thank you."

"I'm officially changing it to Marty Mindfuck."

He was not amused. I didn't care.

After dinner we retired to this cavernous screening room where rushes of the previous night were shown. Sure enough, there I was, grunting away on top of Rhonda. I looked over at Raquel, but she didn't give me the satisfaction of returning my paranoid glare. She seemed entranced by her own performance. Fucking actors.

When it got to my big death scene, I noticed it was cut out or at least obscured by the blue fog machine.

"What do you think?" Marty asked after the house lights went up.

"Nice production values," I said truthfully, "but you lost some crucial plot points in the editing room. Like me getting stabbed in the back."

"That was never filmed, Vic. I don't know what you mean."

"Look, I was there. I felt it. I saw the blood. My blood. Rhonda's blood."

"So where are your wounds?"

"That's what I was wondering, too."

"You just embellished the scene with your imagination, Vic. That's how life is. We all do it, especially in our memories. No recall is ever totally accurate. It's all subjective."

"So, is this still part of your experiment?"

"Experiment? Oh, about figuring out the meaning of life through hypnosis and dreams and all that?"

"Yeah. That."

"Bullshit. Just part of the narrative. That's Raquel's contribution to the script, not mine."

"For which movie? The one we just watched or the one we're in now?

"Both."

"But you did dope my drink and hypnotize me?"

They all laughed, except Raquel. "You drank yourself blind and when we asked you to join our orgy scene, you were more than willing."

"I don't remember that."

"That's your problem. Perhaps you should seek help with your drinking problem, Vic. That's what got you into this situation anyway, in a roundabout way. Is it not?"

I sighed but didn't confirm or deny his hypothesis. Fact was, I was already suffering minor blackouts at the time, which would only grow worse as I got older, resulting in full on fugue states. Perhaps this was an early indicator of my future condition. That's probably why I suppressed it for so long. Not due to trauma. Shame.

I looked over at Raquel, and she looked very sad. I wasn't sure why at the time, besides the fact she lied to me, which was par the course by then, but I was figuring it out on my own.

"Why do all cults always involve sex?" I asked Marty.

"Not the religious ones."

"Especially the religious ones."

"For or against?"

"Both. Either way, it's a common component of these little isolated subcultures. It's always about fear of sex and death. Or a way to justify the act of both in socially taboo ways."

"How would you know? Join many?"

"No, but I've come across a few in my line of work.

Plus, it's California. Cults sprout up around here like rotten avocados."

"You're welcome to remain here as our guest. Consider it compensation for your participation in our film, Vic. Of course, the fact you were one of the stars precludes your from ever divulging this behind-the-scenes peek into our business."

"Does it?"

"It better."

"Or else?"

I heard Dave laughing.

"If I had my gun, you'd all be busted."

"On what charge?"

"Kidnapping, to start."

"Maybe. But you lack the one weapon that could truly help you in this case, Vic."

"What's that?"

"Credibility."

Damn. He had me. It was time for dessert, anyway.

The Hedonists

After dinner everyone went their separate ways. I was supposed to fuck, because what else was there to do around there but sit around watching movies of themselves fucking. Dave had hooked up with Rhonda full time now, and Raquel didn't seem to care, if she ever really did. That left her all for me. Or so I thought.

All the doors were bolted and I couldn't escape, but frankly, I didn't really want to. I was enjoying this vacation, even if the accommodations were like a Playboy Mansion for psychos or Graceland for perverts. After I wandered aimlessly around the opulent dump, gawking at all the velvet paintings of nude Tahitian women and blown-up cheesecake pinup portraits from the Kennedy era, I wound up on the third level and was aroused, literally, by some noise in one of the many bedrooms. I walked in on Martin and Raquel having sweaty sex. I walked out immediately, though I didn't leave once I closed the door behind me. I listened to the moans of pleasure with prurient interest, then some dialogue that shone some bright rays in a few shadowy corners:

"I brought him to make up for Hunter."

"But he's just as resistant."

"I just want to please you."

"You do. But only in a base way. The recruitment is not on schedule."

"What else can I do?"

Then I heard some sounds that both turned me on and repulsed me, so I left.

I ran into Dave wandering the hallway, looking forlorn. He knew what was going on behind closed doors around here, and with whom.

"Hey, why did you beat me up?" I asked him. "Just curious since I don't see your character motivation based on recent revelations."

"I was in character. I'm an actor, just following the script I was given."

"So porn counts?"

"It does when it's part of a larger narrative. These films are made for private investors in the club, and the cause, but they're all top-notch quality."

"Whatever you say, Boogie Nights. So, this whole biker getup is part of the act, too?"

"What? Fuck no. I've been riding motorcycles since I was a teenager. These are my real fucking clothes, asshole. I'm multi-dimensional, unlike you, you fucking film noir cartoon."

"Oh, sorry. Raquel told me you were just playing the part of the biker, for some odd reason."

"No, that part is me."

"So, are you sorry at least? I mean for hitting me."

"Fuck no. That was part of the treatment, I mean for the story. And I'd do it again. Just for kicks. Shit, I might do it again right now if you don't shut the fuck up. Even if you do."

"Don't take it out on me."

"What are you talking about?"

"You know. Raquel and Martin." I nodded toward the sounds of passion emanating from the nearby bedroom. Even I felt a little jealous, since just a little while ago I was voicing the male role in that XXX vignette, with the same female co-star.

"Oh that? I don't care. She fucks whoever she wants, so do I. She's even fucked big ass niggers who stretched out her pussy."

"Um…say what? Raquel said you weren't actually a white supremacist; you just play one on TV."

"I'm not, technically. Not in an ideological sense. But

I'm still a proud white man."

"Okay…wow. More half-truths. Actually, just one-fifth. Anyway, back on topic, why did it bother you so much that she fucked Hunter if you have this ultra-modern sophisticated arrangement?"

He glared at me for a few beats, then said, "She fell in love. That's not part of the deal."

That part of the arrangement I knew to be true, according to Raquel, who wasn't so much a reliable source as a transparent one. There was a rawly primal emotional element linking all these phony narratives that was starting to gel, at least in my semi-professional assessment. More later.

"That's often part of these swinger deals," I said. "I've seen it all in my time as a private eye. Never works. Emotions always kink up the works. It's human nature to be possessive of one's mate, at least for females, many of them, anyway, since they have a womb to think about. Males just want to spread their seed as far and wide as possible in any hole available. That's why I think gay men are generally so promiscuous while there's a proverbial lesbian death bed. Homosexuality is just Nature's preferred method of birth, or rather population control."

"I don't know what the fuck you're talking about."

"Never mind, sorry, I got off on a scientific tangent when really this is about stuff much more visceral and much less academic. Just wondering why emotional commitment matters more to you than sexual monogamy."

"It was for her own protection. Sherry can be very weak. Her tough but smart hick chick routine is just a facade she picked up from Tennessee Williams."

"Tennessee Williams wrote 'Shanty Tramp'?"

"Huh?"

"Not important. Bottom line, if I read you both right even though you're like a script that keeps getting instantly rewritten: Raquel is just a bunch of layers that come unpeeled when it gets too steamy, and you want to keep her from getting hurt. How sweet. You called her Sherry, by the way."

"Sherry was her name when we met. I still think of her as that innocent young girl, before her sister got her mixed up in this pornographic voodoo ring."

"Aren't you?"

"Yeah, for money. Sherry's in it for real. She actually thinks Martin can make a difference. So does Rhonda. Not me. I just like all the loot and loose poon tang."

"You fucked Rhonda, right?"

"Yeah, but it was just animal sex. Hunter fell in love with my woman. I didn't allow it to progress."

"That why he killed himself?"

"No. Bad programming. Got his wires crossed. It happens."

"Programming?"

"We tried to help him. But he was already beholden to different masters."

"Like who? Christ and Hitler and the American flag?"

"Those don't even go together."

"No ideally. Just wondering, since we had a conversation before he died. I don't think he was a Nazi, though. I just threw that in to get your reaction."

"You saying I am?"

I nodded at the swastika on his hand.

"Oh that? Just to scare people. Part of the act."

"For what purpose? I mean why scare anyone?"

"It's the role I've been assigned. I don't ask questions."

"Assigned? By who? Marty Mephisto?"

"Don't call him that."

"Why don't you just leave?"

"Why don't you?"

"Doors and windows are all locked from the outside, last I checked. Plus, I lost my driver's license. Waiting for Raquel. She's my ride, though right now she's riding your director."

Then he punched me, hard. I fell and shook it off, but he just walked away. I guess I hit a nerve. He just hit my face. Again. And my blood wasn't actually ketchup, I assure you. If I'd had my gun, I would've shot him with a real bullet. I just didn't give a damn anymore.

"I love fucking her too!" I yelled after him, but he didn't even turn around, just kept walking away while flashing me a middle finger. Truth was, it was just sex between Raquel and me. Only love spoiled everything.

I got up, shook off my latest fist-induced daze, and continued snooping around the joint.

That's when I found the pictures.

After I didn't shoot Buck/Dave/Whoever the Fuck, I started randomly opening doors. Most were locked. One wasn't. I wish it had been.

There were stacks of boxes neatly piled on top of each other. I popped one open and inside were dozens of Polaroids depicting extreme carnage. After I flipped through a dozen or so shots of human entrails and brains,

I got to one where Raquel had blood dripping from her chin and down her nude breasts as she munched on what appeared to be a human heart.

My own heart starting racing for the door, but my perverse fascination wouldn't let the rest of me follow. Other shots revealed that every person I had met in this hellhole was indeed a fucking cannibal.

I wasn't sure whether I should confront any of them. I was afraid I was an upcoming menu item and I didn't want to entice them into serving me earlier than planned. I stuck a few pictures in my pocket, including the one of Raquel, and shut the door, shivering from shock.

Of course, who should I run across in the hallway but Rhonda, wearing a tiger print bikini even though there was no indoor pool, with black pumps.

"Can I help you, Vic?"

"We fucked already, so no."

"Yes, I noticed that."

"You noticed?"

"In the film."

"You were there, though."

"Yes, but I guess I blanked it out."

"Wow. Okay, well, see you at dinner…"

I tried to walk past her, but a Polaroid fell out of my pocket. She picked it up, looked at it, and laughed.

"Oh, I see you found these! I must've forgotten to lock that closet again, silly me."

"You're fucking cannibals!" I blurted out.

She laughed again. "Vic, this was for a film! This is all fake!"

"Looks real to me."

"We hire good special effects people."

"I don't believe you."

"What are you going to do, call the cops?"

"Maybe."

"Try it. Remember you skipped out on them up in Frisco, so they probably have a warrant out for your arrest."

"I don't care. I'm busting this cannibal porn snuff film racket wide open. And don't call it Frisco."

She laughed again, and actually handed the picture back to me. "You're gonna need this, then. Good luck!"

Then she walked away, laughing. She remained an enigma to me up until and beyond the end of this strange experience. I still enjoyed fucking her, though.

Right after this encounter I saw Raquel coming out of Marty's room, so I confronted her next, sticking the incriminating picture of her right in her face.

At first her expression was one of revulsion, but then she squinted at the photo some more and laughed. "Oh my god, I forgot all about that party!"

"Party? Rhonda just told me it was for a film."

"Oh, the fake body parts were. This was the wrap party. See you at dinner, Vic. I'm spent. Martin wore me out, sorry."

That was probably meant to bother and distract me, and it did. In any case, I was really glad I passed on the beef. I continued to do so at dinner that night, eyeing all the entrees with renewed suspicion, but nobody cracked. They were one solid ensemble; I'll give them that much credit. My biggest fear was that they were actually really good actors. Too good for my own good.

I wound up staying the rest of the week, fucking and eating, keeping a close watch on my hosts/captors. I fucked Rhonda once more, but she seemed really bored, so mostly I just fucked Raquel, who was much more enthusiastic. Dave didn't give a fuck, either, though I wish he did, just so I could needle him. He seemed content to fuck Rhonda and a couple other of the cultists, basically the nameless movie extras. I thought about going for it with them, but I was content with Raquel and really I'm not that big of a slut out in the real world. One woman at a time is plenty for me, if I get even that lucky, and right now, I felt lucky as hell, so I just went with it.

It made me a little sick to think I was sharing the same women with Dave and Marty, but I was in proverbial sex haze and wasn't feeling especially picky or judicious. After a while I gave up the notion they were cannibal pornographers due to lack of corroborating evidence and also, like I said, I was in a sex haze and just didn't care. That possibility just seemed too crazy, even for them, though that odd remark Hunter made back at The Drive-Inn, about cannibalism being a "trigger" for him, still bugged me. But a lot of things bug me. I just learn to live with them.

I did a lot of thinking when not eating or drinking or fucking. Not much talking since I couldn't trust anything anyone said anyway. I kept my thoughts to myself this time, at least until I had them all organized in my own head, and they finally began to make sense.

Also, the time I wasted overindulging my senses without outside intervention or internal judgement— rather encouragement—made me understand the appeal of belonging to a cult. It's not just the indoctrination. It's the insulation. It's a way to be non-conformist but also accepted, to have your most radical desires and ideas validated by peers who share your perspective. But I don't ultimately trust anything organized that enforces group-think, whether it's a cult or religion or corporation or sports team or political party or country club. Easier to just break off from the pack, any pack, and go my own way, make my own choices and mistakes. I never did like anyone telling me what to think or do. I never respected authority, especially when self-appointed.

Maybe that's my problem. I don't know because I never listen to anyone but me. And I'm a bona fide sex addict. I've even been in a program to treat it. It didn't take. Because I didn't want to let go of my addiction. Only now, in a happy marriage, am I finally "cured." But that's also due to the fact my dick is nothing but tofu jerky these days. Sometimes the only cure for any problem is the one solution we resist the most: the relentless and merciless passage of time.

One night after a particularly therapeutic sex session, which I couldn't wait to tell Dave about, I confronted Raquel again. This time with what I knew to be true, following intense contemplation of the few facts I knew up to that point, separating the wheat from the chaff, or maybe just the poison ivy from the cow manure:

"I just thought of something," I said for a start.

"Yes?"

"You're not pregnant, with anyone's baby."

"What made you think I was?"

"You said you might be knocked up by Hunter, way back on the road down."

"Oh, right. Sorry, I can't always keep my stories straight."

"I noticed. Marty Mindfuck blew your cover."

"It's not a cover. It's what I choose to believe, regardless of what he says."

"But isn't he the director?"

"Of our collective experimental movie, not my real life."

"The difference being?"

"The lines are blurry, I admit. I'm not always sure where they are anymore."

"I wish my life was a movie. I mean for real. It would make things so much simpler."

"Yeah? Which movie would it be?"

"I don't know. Ideally? *The Maltese Falcon*. But then I'd have to be a real detective like Sam Spade, not just a guy that pretends to be one based on something he saw in an old movie."

"As I recall, the girl he's in love with doesn't end up so well in that one."

"That's what she gets for changing her stories so many times and messing with his head."

"Good thing we're not in love."

"Good thing. But then you're already in love, aren't you?"

"Yes. I wish I was pregnant with his child, Vic. Then maybe he'd still be alive. He'd have something to live for, besides me."

"I think you mean he'd feel obligated to stay with you,

out of commitment to the kid, right?"

She looked away, tears immediately forming in her eyes. I finally had her in a rare moment of naked honesty, as it were. So, I took advantage of her vulnerability and went in for the kill:

"I've been doing a lot of thinking about this epic mess and have reached some conclusions I want to run by you. Let me say all this back to you to make sure we both have these interconnected shifting stories straight, finally."

"Okay..." Her trepidation was palpable as she braced herself for the blitz of truth, which meant she already knew I had her nailed.

"Your half-sister Rhonda actually is a Satanist and a stripper and a prostitute. Dave is actually a biker, as well as an actor, just not a Hell's Angel. He's also a bigot but that's incidental. And you're actually from Texas, also an actress. Not a stripper or prostitute. Just a promiscuous part time private porn star for hire. You and Hunter were in love, or you were, but then he cheated on you with Rhonda, so you got back at him by sleeping with his best friend Buck—whose real name is Dave, not Buck, which was a cover alias when he decided to try his hand at acting.

"Turns out it was these professionally produced pseudo-snuff flicks made by Marty Mephisto, real name Martin Devlin, from what I read around here when no one was looking. After your sister introduced you to him, Martin recruited you and Dave to star in his 'industrial films' which he sold to the rich and perverted. Hunter turned him down because of his religious background, which to your dismay was starting to influence his thinking again. The whole experience down here reignited his passion for Christ so he was born again again, which meant no more sex or drugs or any of the fun stuff. You resented this since he came to Jesus after he came inside your sister, and she jilted him. You saw his return to his religious roots as a reaction to this rejection, not to you partaking in private porn movies, some of which included actual murders, but you said you didn't know they were real and I'll go ahead and believe you even though you haven't really earned the benefit of the doubt. Then I was duped and dragged into this triple X-rated psycho-drama so you'd have company for your misery. Now Dave and your sister have become casualties of this profit-driven porn party. Is that a fair rundown?"

"Yes," she said simply after, shall we say, a pregnant pause. "That's about the size of it. I mean, some of the details are different, since as you know I invent various backstories just so I can stand living in my own skin, but they don't matter. Basically, that's the whole entire truth. I mean, mostly. I'm so sorry, Vic."

She was crying softly and hell, so was I. I really liked her. More like I felt sorry for her. And of course, I was still attracted to her. But all of her deceit and deception and multiple assumed identities had alienated my heart. But my heart still hurt for her. Just not in a romantic way, which was always selfish. This time I just wanted her to be happy, even if she didn't deserve it. Who does and doesn't deserve happiness is not my call, though. If I was in a position to provide it, maybe I should. Except my conscience kept nagging me, and there's no more effective party pooper like a Goddamned conscience. She deserved a break anyway, I thought, even if she did kill Hunter. It wasn't really her fault. Right? I just didn't know that particular answer right away, and it was to the only question that counted. So, I asked another one I already knew the answer to:

"You don't like yourself very much, do you?" I said, trying a little tenderness.

"No. That's why I keep hiding beneath all these masks, all these layers. It's like I can only be myself if I'm pretending to be someone else."

"Sad."

"Yes. It is."

"You're not alone, though."

"Not in here, I'm not."

I nodded. No point in arguing with the truth. I didn't always like myself, either. But I didn't know how to be anyone else but me. I was stuck with myself. I almost envied her creative identity emancipation, even if it was a perpetual delusion.

I thought of her as a young girl, and me a young man, even though I was born too old for her. But say our souls had synced up in time and space, and we'd met one night on a train in Europe or someplace romantic and spent the whole night talking and then making love, promising to rendezvous back here in six months no matter what for a reunion that could lead to a lifetime of love. That was only a story in a movie I'd seen. But it still resonated with me. I could see Raquel as that young girl on the train, innocent and free, before her demons destroyed her and any chance she had for happiness. I could've been her guardian angel. Maybe I still could.

Then utter chaos ensued. I heard a bullhorn blaring authoritarian bluster from out front of the mansion. Marty Mindfuck and his tribe of thespian whores had finally been busted. It might've been that dime I dropped earlier that day. I can't be sure since when I dialed 911, I was put on hold and then disconnected. I just assumed they traced the call. I also assumed nobody could get away with such an elaborate set-up forever. In any case, Raquel was in a panic as we threw on our clothes and ran downstairs, where Marty, Dave and the gang were suddenly all gunned up, strapped to the teeth with sophisticated firearms.

Money can buy anything in show business if you have a big enough budget.

The place was surrounded by a SWAT team, apparently. Bullets tore through the windows. Tear gas exploded and imbued the chaotic violence with an eerie, dreamy beauty, but then I was safe from the onslaught, hiding with Raquel in a downstairs closet. After a while I could only hear what was happening, but I saw enough.

Once the cops announced their presence and ordered the immediate surrender of everyone inside, Dave pulled out a shotgun and opened fire out a window rather randomly. Through bleary eyes and the crack of a door I saw him get ripped apart by snipers before a battering ram knocked down the front door. More bullets flew back and forth. Rhonda became another gory casualty, her bikini-clad body all bloodied up, even though she was unarmed, simply running around on high heels screaming as her fellow cultists tried to hold down the fort against the onslaught.

This is how I remember it: bodies getting blown away in slow motion a la Sam Peckinpah and John Woo. I can't testify they all got killed, even Dave and Rhonda. I just know what I perceived, and I never saw or heard from them again. That's as good as being dead, from a subjective viewpoint. We're only alive if we have witnesses.

Once the smoke cleared, Raquel and I were found and led away by the cops, but not cuffed. Oddly, the tear gas had no effect on us, which didn't really hit me till later, when I was mentally sorting this all out. LAPD actually let us go, since we were both in the wrong place at the wrong time, they determined. Plus, we weren't black, so there was that. I'd have quite a story to tell my pals at SFPD when I got back. But I never told them about this experience. I never told them anything, with one exception.

On the way out I looked at Marty Mephisto, who had been wounded in the raid. I swear his eyes turned a glowing red as he smiled at me. I guess I'll never know for sure. I'll also never know if all the cops and paramedics were actors, and this whole scene was the big action set piece they'd been saving for the finale. I asked Raquel because I knew she'd be straight with me. That was a joke.

"If I told you this whole thing, including the gun fight and deaths, was elaborately staged and faked by actual cannibalistic Satanic snuff porn producers with rich clients just to throw you off their track, since those photographs were real and incriminating and had to be destroyed after you found them, but if you tried to tell anyone what happened you'd have no evidence and they'd just laugh at you, and the gun fight was filmed as part of the porn movie you unwittingly participated in, but considering you have no proof and no power, and you're already in a jam with the law yourself, would it really make any difference?"

I let out a big sigh. I was burnt out by then and wanted it all to be over. "None. Fuck this. Let's go home. My home, anyway."

We drove back north toward an uncertain destination. Same as everyone. Except we took the scenic route. Because why not.

We didn't talk much, but she was in mourning. And not for Dave or even her sister. I know she was pretty much over Dave, but I asked her if her sister's violent death bothered her. She shrugged nonchalantly. "We were estranged anyway." She just didn't forgive Rhonda for fucking Hunter. Maybe they'd get together in the hereafter and have the last laugh, or last fuck. If Rhonda was really dead. Raquel sure wasn't acting like it. I wondered if the raid on the mansion was indeed just another big budget con job, like everything else I'd witnessed there, despite its realism. Raquel refused to discuss it any further, seemingly preoccupied with something else.

As usual, I got the idea she knew something I didn't.

Yet.

Hallelujah

"What made you suddenly remember of all this?" my wife Val asked me while sitting on that bench in Ravenna Park. We had just returned from a vacation in the San Juan Islands.

"Remember we were in Friday Harbor and we witnessed that accident?"

"You mean the guy who got hit in the crosswalk?"

"Yeah."

"But he got up and walked away. He was fine."

"I know. But for some reason this whole case flashed back in my brain. I had completely blocked it out."

"Why, do you think?"

"I guess because of how it ended. Plus, it's traumatic to kill someone, even by accident. I still feel like it was my fault since I was a bit tipsy, and I wasn't concentrating on the road." I left out the part where I felt ashamed about my extended stay in the sex mansion.

"Everyone looks down to fiddle with the radio sometimes."

"I know, and this is the worst possible outcome of that common distraction."

"But you know now it wasn't your fault."

"Still, it's scary how quickly your life can change. You can go from being a good guy to a bad guy in a second, all your decent deeds washed away and replaced by a single callous act that results in a fatality, for which you will be punished for the rest of your days. From that split second, your existence amounts to nothing more than that singe mistake."

"But you're not a bad guy, Vic. You didn't get punished because you did nothing wrong, not really. You are basically a good guy, Vic. Fundamentally we don't change, no matter how much we lie to each other, or ourselves."

"So, some people are basically bad?"

"Essentially, maybe, though maybe through no fault of their own. We all make choices, Vic. Some people are put in a more difficult position than others when it comes to life decisions. Many just have it harder than the rest."

"Like Hunter."

"Maybe."

"Like Raquel."

"Definitely. If that was even her name. Did you ever find out who she really was?"

"I don't know. I don't even know if she ever found out who she was."

"I think she knew but didn't want to accept it."

"You really think we're capable of change?"

"Attitudes and behavior? Reactions to circumstances beyond our control and personal growth? Absolutely. But at our core, regardless of our decisions, I think our souls remain the same. We're born with a core identity. The rest is environment and free will."

"But what dictates these decisions if not our true personality?"

"Impulses, greed, lust, stupidity. We often go against our own natures whether due to desperation, fear, tribalism...or love."

"Yeah. I keep thinking of Raquel, and you, and Monica,

and Rose, and all the women I've been with, before they, even you, got corrupted by the world. I think of myself in the same way. I think of little girls I'd sneak a kiss with when I was a little boy, how innocent and thrilling it was, but also sad because on the one hand everything felt like forever but then reality would intercede, they'd move away or lose interest or you would, and gradually the concept of eternity gave way to inevitable change and spiritual corrosion and moral compromise. Basically, we all get cynical after a while."

"You just never gave up on the pursuit of falling in love with the same passion you experienced when you were young, when you first met Rose, for instance."

"Like in "Before Sunset.'"

"Exactly. But don't forget that was a trilogy. Richard Linklater was really exploring the ravages of time, not just the evolution and ultimate dissolution of young love."

"What about us?"

"Our love developed and strengthened over time, via experience and mutual respect and physical attraction. I loved you from afar for a long time, Vic. But that was only a projection. And you feel like you conjured me out of your deepest carnal feminine fantasies."

"Sometimes I do feel like I'm talking to myself. No, you know what I mean. I can't shake the feeling you're just a phantom I invented to keep me company."

"Like a childhood imaginary friend?"

"Except I'm no child."

"And I'm not imaginary."

"But you are my friend."

"The best, I hope."

"Yes, best ever, next to Doc. But he and I never fucked." I also thought of Monica, how we were best friends at one point who had great sex, but I just didn't have that youthful ache when we kissed. I don't have it now with Val. But I have something much closer to that boyhood sensation of serene stasis. Maybe it's just early senility.

"Anyway, I'm glad you shared this story with me," Val said. "Even if it does seem like you filled in a lot of blanks with shit you saw in old horror movies."

"Maybe. I mean, I'm relating stuff Raquel told me too, and she kept changing her story, so I can't be sure what was real and what wasn't, even from her perspective. I don't even know if this memory was suppressed due to emotional stress, or I really was hypnotized into forgetting it once it ended. The whole episode started and ended in about a week. Just a fraction of my life. And yet it left a psychic impression on me, subconsciously influenced other decisions, and impacted other experiences of mine further down the road."

"So do you feel a sense of catharsis now that you've finally remembered and revisited it, even if was revised in your memory and imagination?"

"I don't know. I feel like in my shattered kaleidoscope, memories of other cases, other events, other people, characters, and scenes in movies mingled and merged along with chance encounters with strangers in strange dreams. I can't really tell you what actually happened versus what might've happened or didn't happen or maybe happened in a different time and place with different people, and I'm confusing them."

"How do you mean?"

"Well, this one case I just told you about seemed like a mashup of several other cases I had a few years before. Like a mystery woman I'm involved with who blows me just to keep me in check and deflect from the reality of the relationship. That was the same M.O. used to my detriment but with my horny stupid consent by my junkie hooker high school sweetheart, Dolly Duncan Dunlap."

"The doper dentist's dame who had an affair with your father then shot him dead in an alley."

"That's the one. And the whole sex cult was eerily reminiscent of Deacon Rivers and his Church of Elvis. And then me being filmed without my knowledge for a secret movie was just like the time Doc and I went to L.A. and got mixed up with that crooked politician who ran a similar clandestine underground guerrilla film operation that happened to star both of us for his own twisted amusement. I can't help thinking these last three are all connected somehow."

"If only in your mind?"

"That's the true mystery of life, the one mystery I could never crack, the whole reason I became a private eye to begin with. The mystery of love and life and death and all that jazz. I can't even be sure my memories are of actual events or just flights of fantasy or somewhere in between. I guess I'm an epic failure when it comes to my one real mission in life."

"You're still on the case, Vic. You're still here. And we found each other. We have love. Unlike Hunter. Or

Raquel."

"Yeah. She acted strangely, at least to me, for a woman in love. It seemed to be more about possession. Not demonic possession. Romantic obsession. In a way, she imbued Hunter with all her yearning, all her loneliness, all the things Dave and Martin and a thespian sex cult—or Satanic cannibal porn ring, take your pick—couldn't fulfill. But then neither could Hunter in the end. And I think that rejection sent her over the edge. I just happened to be there to catch her fall. Only I was off by just a little bit, but just enough."

"She's dead?"

"I don't know, but last time I saw her, the look on her face was one of defeat. That often leads to surrender and then, well, demise. First spiritually and then literally."

"Whatever happened to her? You still haven't told me how this all turned out. I'm assuming she talked to the police and they let you off the hook."

"Yes. And no."

"I hate those bullshit noncommittal answers. Just give it to me straight, Vic. As straight as you can shoot, anyway."

"Okay. But one more thing that just hit me: the denouement of this sad, sordid little nightmare echoes the case that brought me here to Seattle for good."

"Raven, the burlesque star who turned out to be the true culprit in that case."

"Yeah."

"Okay, now I'm really curious. Lay it on me, daddy-o."

So, I told Val what I'm about to tell you, and everything after the colon I remember with crystal clarity as if it happened yesterday. Trust me:

Raquel dropped me off at The Drive-Inn. It was late but I knew it was still open since it was a Saturday. Not many people inside, but that was good. I just wanted to be alone with my pal.

Doc was playing the 1968 Mexican superhero monster flick *La Mujer Murcielago*, AKA *The Batwoman*, a personal favorite. It felt better than ever to be home. Now if only I could find a way to stay here. I still wasn't sure Raquel would come through for me. To say she was unpredictable was an understatement.

"You don't seem to have much to say, Vic," Doc said, disappointed.

"Sorry, Doc. This has been the single weirdest week of my life."

"You sound like Bruce Willis in *Pulp Fiction*."

"Except I'm not Bruce Willis, you're not Ving Rhames, this ain't *Pulp Fiction*, but my week was still fucking weirder than anything in that movie or any movie. Anyway, I feel more like Mickey Rourke in *Angel Heart*."

"You want to talk about it?"

"No."

"Later?"

"Never."

"You straighten your situation out with the cops at least?"

"That's pending. But don't worry. I will."

"I never really worry about you, Vic. If nothing else, you're resilient."

"Thanks, Doc. I'm too consumed by self-loathing to appreciate the compliment right now, though."

"I don't do compliments for their own sake, Vic. Flattery gets me nowhere. I'm just calling it like I see it. Nobody but Monica knows you better than me. You are who you are."

"Yeah. We all are, I guess."

And that's exactly what bothered me, but I didn't tell Doc that. I didn't tell him anything. I wish I had. If I could talk to anyone right now, it would be Doc. My wife Val has assumed his role as my advisor and confidant, but she can never replace him, just like she can never be replaced. Every person in our lives plays a unique part in the drama of our brief existence. I cherish them all, even the ones I didn't like, because I'll never see them again once it's all over, and that makes me sad. I hope we have souls, so I'll see Doc again in that big Drive-Inn in the sky, or wherever it is.

After my weekly therapy session with Doc, such as it was, I went up to my room and watched the Wes Anderson movie *Bottle Rocket*. Another recent movie about being young and foolish. I was relatively young at the time, even though I already felt old. Now that I'm actually old, I'm nostalgic for when I just felt old compared to people who were actually young. It's all fucking relative. So relative it makes me nauseous.

After the movie I just lay there, thinking. I won't tell you what I was thinking yet, but you'll figure it out. Suffice to say my thoughts were disturbing and kept me awake for most of the night.

The next day around noon I called Raquel because I had something I needed to say to her. Plus, I wanted to know when she'd come clean with the cops and release me from this curse.

"I guess I'm ready," she said in a soft, faraway voice that made my gut feel like a meat grinder.

"You guess? Baby, I need you to tell the truth, to the right people, not just for my sake, but for yours. Otherwise, I might be forced to tell the truth, and that may help me, but it definitely won't help you."

"What the hell are you talking about?"

"I think you pushed him," I said. "You were hurt, angry, jealous because of his relationship with your sister, for lying to you that he believed in your cause, even if you were lying, too. He betrayed you by not believing your fantasy. And by sleeping with your sister, but that was the lesser of his sins. His worst offense was not loving you back as much as you loved him."

There was another of her pregnant pauses, until she finally admitted in a whisper, "Yes. I pushed him, just a little, out of sheer frustration, not meaning to kill him, but I did anyway. It was just a monetary impulse with unintended consequences. I felt guilty, so I wanted to help you. I still can."

"I know. I'm calling the cops on myself right now, letting them know I'm back in town. I'm sure they have a warrant for my arrest for leaving town, even if I was kidnapped."

"If I tell them I kidnapped you, will I get in trouble?"

"Of course. You interfered directly with an investigation. That's against the law in polite society. Not that anyone is very polite in the circles that surround us."

"Despite my layers of subterfuge, Vic, I'm the same person I always was. It just took you a while to know who

I really am."

"Do you?"

"People change their clothes and names and circumstances, Vic. But they can't change their souls."

"I agree. We are who we are. But you still killed an innocent man, even if it was a crime of passion."

"All I want is a chance to redeem myself. The truth won't set me free. Not in this case."

"But a lie can set you free."

"Both of us. It will set both of us free. Let's just stick with the original story, that Hunter killed himself. I saw him jump in front of your car while you were preoccupied with the radio, only I couldn't tell what it was exactly. But you'll fill in that detail. You were distracted turning the dial, and Hunter took advantage and ran in front of the car. You were going just fast enough to kill him."

"I was legally drunk, too."

"That doesn't change the fact he wouldn't have been in a position to get run over by you unless he'd made that leap himself."

"Listen, how do I know this just isn't another improv scene at my expense?"

"I swear, Vic. This is the truth. This is really me talking. Sherry Ann Baker of Long Beach, California. You can look that up."

"Long Beach? You never mentioned that before."

"Because I was playing a complex part. This is my true back story. You can verify it. I just need to finally be real with someone. I'm glad it's you, Vic."

I thought about it a bit, then said, "Okay. How soon can

you get here?"

She told me and it synced with the ETA of the cops, close enough anyway, and the rendezvous was arranged. We'd end all of this once and for all, one way or another.

The cops had me cuffed in custody already when she showed up and told them she could provide a signed affidavit that Hunter killed himself, though she had no concrete evidence. Still, eyewitness testimony that he lunged in front of the car would probably suffice, so once again, I was released on my own recognizance.

That's when I had a decision to make, one I regret to this day. In a nearby apartment, someone had their window open and Jeff Buckley was singing "Hallelujah." I'll never forget that, even if it never actually happened.

"I'm sorry, Raquel," I said, sincerely but ineffectually. Then I said to my old pals, Police Detectives Sharp and Shoemaker: "Actually, Hunter Thompson didn't jump in front of my car. He was pushed. By her, in a fit of romantic rage, so it wasn't strictly a homicide, involuntary manslaughter at worst, if you want to get technical. In any case, I have her full confession on tape."

That's when I produced the cassette I'd used to record our conversation over the phone.

She looked at me with cold, pitiful resignation and said, "These corrupt people with absolute authority are the true evil. Because they don't really care about morals or freedom or real people like you and me. Only about their job security and enforcing laws to control us with no mercy or redemption. And now you're one of them, too. You've sold your soul after all, Vic."

"Maybe I'll get it back some day," I said, tears in my

eyes, reflecting her own. "I'll redeem myself if I keep telling the truth, at least as I know it. I'm thinking of justice for Hunter too, not just you and me."

In my head I was already trying to justify my decision to betray her trust. The fact she'd betrayed mine multiple times didn't matter, since in the end she did right by me. They'd probably let her off easy since not only was his death the result of an ill-timed impulse—hers, not mine or his—but as far as I knew, she had no priors, unless she really was a Satanic cannibalistic porn star. Of course, none of that jazz was actually illegal, unless she indeed killed a real person for consumption, or aided and abetted their murders. I still never really knew her, just like I never knew Hunter: their childhoods, their backgrounds, all the stuff that made them who they were when I crossed their paths and inadvertently changed their lives forever, and not for the better. I never followed up and never found out and now it's too late.

But her fate, and her departing words, keep haunting me, just like the soul of Hunter calling me a loser over and over and over in my nightmares:

"You sold your soul, Vic," she said again as she was cuffed.

"I'll get it back," I said without conviction, suddenly feeling like what I hate most: a conformist. "Someday."

She was naturally upset and so I disregarded her hyperbole in the moment. Fact was, I traded a soul for a conscience. But I wasn't sure whose soul was lost in the bargain.

"No refunds on souls," she said to me as the cops led her away.

PANTY-STUFFED SNAKESKIN SHOE

A Vic Valentine Vignette

There's a lesson in this somewhere, one I doubt I'll ever learn. I should add that due to my prolonged series of fugue states (more or less self diagnosed), I can't even verify the veracity of this vignette. I rely mostly on muscle memory to navigate this fever dream called Life. The trouble is my brain isn't very muscular.

I will provide as many incidental details as possible to prove I was at least paying attention.

For a fact I was at Fenway Park, during a recent trip to Boston with my magical wife Val, short for Ava Margarita Esmeralda Valentina Valdez. If you know my history, it seems improbable that a brilliant, sensuous Latina bombshell with a PhD in Basically Everything would even notice much less marry a washed up ex-private eye who learned everything he knew about his profession from old movies. I guess I got lucky.

I'd been to Boston a couple of times as a kid with my parents. Those were some good times before all the tragedies hit in slow succession: My old man was a dirty cop found dead in an alley (murdered by someone I loved), my old lady a mentally disturbed beauty who died in an institution, and my depressed older brother jumped off the Brooklyn Bridge as a teenager. I didn't get this way by accident. It's divine design. I was meant to be a mess.

This trip to Boston was the latest in a series of therapeutic measures my patient wife took to treat if not cure my ongoing mental malaise. She also had a speaking engagement at Harvard, which I skipped while exploring Cambridge for the first time. As a high school dropout I felt out of place in the high-falutin' collegiate environment, pleasant as it was. My favorite spot there was a tiki bar called Wusong Road. That was our first night. The next night we had Asian food and Mai Tais at the legendary Kowloon down in Saugus, an old school exotic restaurant with giant tiki statues and fountains and the ambience of 1950s tropical resort. It was another place I'd visited as a kid with my family. Now Val was my family. She was also my only friend, ever since Doc died. He was the owner of The Drive-Inn, a combo bar/video store back in San Francisco, where my so-called career started. Doc is still with me in spirit, though.

At the Kowloon, Val and I talked about her personal history in the area, particularly Salem. She'd once lived there for a brief time, which was news to me, and wanted to look up some old friends that "dabbled in the dark arts." I was game.

The following day I agreed to see a ballgame with her at Fenway as a token of my gratitude. Our pricey seats right behind home plate were totally wasted on me. As I've said before I was never a sports fan because I'm not athletic, competitive, or tribalistic. But my wife liked baseball. No particular team but in this case she was rooting for the Oakland A's, just to piss off the Red Sox fans. I wasn't worried. If she got into a fight, she could take care of herself. She was an expert martial artist on top of everything else. I was just tagging along as a gofer, not a bodyguard.

Soon after getting seated I left to buy a couple of meatless hot dogs (we're both vegan) at the one concession stand that advertised them, waiting in a long line before being told they were all out. Story of my life. Maybe it was because I was dressed like a Rat Pack reject, not just another conformist Clyde marching lockstep in the parade of banality. I asked this guy wearing a red shirt where I could score vegan food. He gave me a quizzical, condescending look and told me to try this open air area where kids play, which I'd normally avoid like a toxic dump. I checked it out and didn't see any vegan options on any menus around there.

Next I asked someone else in a red shirt (they'd all be dead soon if this was Star Trek, fine with me) and he sent me to the "Information" booth. There I was told about a stand called Mings Bings that offered vegan dogs and other plant-based bullshit two flights straight up, on level four. I went up, looked all over, and didn't see any MingsBings. I asked around and no one had heard of it, not even the elevator operators. I even checked on level three. Nada. So I returned to the Info booth. They swore it was there and to try again. I did that. It still was nowhere to be found and still no one had ever heard of it. I asked some old guy at the nearest entry gate and he said it was back by home plate, where I came from. Tried again, still couldn't find it. For some reason the vintage instrumental "Moon Mist" by the Blue Jeans was blaring inside my head throughout this entire experience. It was so loud I wondered if anyone heard it but me.

I went back to the original concession stand that allegedly sold vegan dogs and asked someone there if they knew of MingsBings. Nope. But then this person asked her manager, who had actually heard of it and tried sending me back to Fenway's version of the Twilight Zone department store on level four. I told him I'd already been there and not only could I not find it but no one working in that section had ever even heard of it. So he called someone up there to confirm. I saw him nodding and then he hung up and told me to go back to the Info booth and ask for some joker named Jake, who would personally escort me to the mythical MingsBings. I did.

No one there knew who the hell Jake was.

Whatever. Back in Seattle, we often had vegan hot dogs when Val dragged me to a Mariners game. I missed Seattle, even if the residents were both the worst dressers and worst drivers in the world.

The upshot was I had to go back to Val empty handed.

When I got back to our seats, she was gone. I waited a while before I called her cellphone. Someone answered that wasn't her and told me I had the wrong number. My stomach clenched into tumorous knots.

"Have you seen my wife?" I asked the people sitting

around me, all wearing unfriendly Red Sox gear. Everyone shook their head. Val looked like a Russ Meyer Supervixen, hard to miss or forget. Everyone insisted I'd been there alone the entire time. I figured they were messing with me because she'd been cheering on the opposing team.

I waited until the game ended, but she never showed up. There had to be an explanation. Probably not a rational one.

I walked back to where we were staying, The Verb Hotel on the immediate outskirts of the ballpark. The decor was very colorful and midcentury retro, like a '60s Batman villain lair, with a vintage LP theme and pool that made it feel like you were in Palm Springs. Lots of hip bands stayed there. I was half hoping to run into Debbie Harry in the hallway. Before I lost my wife, that is. Good to have backup though.

I went into our room and found none of her clothes or makeup or toiletries there. Just a single high-heeled snakeskin strappy shoe. For some reason, her leopard print panties were stuffed inside of it. But that was it. No signs of a struggle. No note. It was like she was never there, in that room.

Or on this planet, outside my own head.

Of course, the private eye ghost inside me considered the worst, that she'd been abducted or worse, she'd abandoned me. If she'd been kidnapped, I'd go into my former crime-busting mode and this would be a thrilling adventure ending in a triumphant reunion. If she simply left me, which seemed more probable given my unworthiness, it would be just another soul-crushing, heartbreaking coda to a lonely, pointless existence. I could've just called the cops, but the problem was I had no photos of Val on me, or any tangible evidence of her existence. Except this shoe.

Anyway, my experience was I was better off tracking her down myself. After all, I became a private eye to find a long lost love, years ago. I didn't find her but she found me. It didn't work out. Her name was Rose by then, but when I knew her back in the day, it was Valerie. I called her Val. Coincidence. If you believe in those.

After the desk clerk told me I'd checked in alone, which was a lie, I began wandering aimlessly around downtown Boston, looking for a woman who was my wife, at least from my point of view. I carried the snakeskin shoe under one arm and stuffed the leopard print panties inside my sharkskin jacket. I was on existential safari. As long as I had these physical items, I knew she had once and still existed outside the dimension of my own dementia. I needed to see her again, even if no one else could. She was my only connection to everyone else's reality, the one I allegedly inhabited.

After walking up and down the brick sidewalks of Beacon Hill, wondering what it would be like to live in one of those cool old row houses, ensconced in vivid history and shadowy tree shade, I followed the Freedom Trail, starting at the Common and winding up at Quincy Market. I dug all the dinosaur statues. Reminded me of being a kid, when the benevolent dream world you envisioned in your mind felt just as real as the one that you physically felt, that hurt and let you down. At a

Mexican cantina called Mija in Faneuil Hall I sat at the outdoor bar and ordered a Margarita. One of Val's many middle names.

Then I remembered our conversation back at the Kowloon.

I took a cab to North Station and caught a red line train directly to Salem. It was twilight when I arrived. I was immediately intrigued by the innate Halloween atmosphere. I walked along Essex Street checking out the spooky shops and monster museums, lost in a nostalgic haze, remembering all the horror movies I'd watched with my brother as kids. I figured I'd get the tourist crap out of the way since I was probably just chasing down another delusion anyway.

The crisp, early autumn breeze sweetened my senses. I strolled past the famous witch cemetery without whistling since I can't whistle and walked up Derby Street. There I saw a retro neon bar sign that read All Souls Lounge.

This reminded me of something someone sad once said to me, "No refunds on souls." Though when I told Val about it, she revised it in response as "All souls are final."

Taking this as a cosmic clue I went inside. It was a dark, cozy joint with hardwood floors and brick walls. I sat down at the bar and ordered a dirty Martini. Sinatra was singing "Witchcraft" from the eclectic jukebox. Despite my despair I felt at peace for the first time in ages. This was a good place to disappear.

That's when I looked down and saw a single snakeskin shoe, the companion to the one sitting on the bar next to my drink. Inside of it was a mustard-stained paper wrapper that read "MingsBings."

I asked the bartender if he knew who belonged to the shoe and he had no idea, but he figured it was mine since I had the other one. I didn't get into it. Instead I asked for a recommendation for a place to crash while in town. He suggested the nearby Hawthorne Hotel, which was apparently haunted. Like me. I finished my Martini as Frank sang "That Old Black Magic."

Walking through the grandiose, chandelier-illuminated lobby past a beckoning wood-paneled tavern, I looked into an ornate mirror on the far wall. I saw Val's reflection following me, but not my own, like I was a vampire, though her floating shoes and panties were visible. She was wearing only her leopard print bra, nothing else. No one but me seemed to notice. I didn't care. At least neither of us was alone anymore.

She sat on a plush sofa as I put both snakeskin shoes on her feet, then she stood up and slipped on the leopard print panties. Everything was back in its proper place. My universe was once again complete.

That's when it all made sense. I hadn't conjured her. She'd conjured me.

Made in the USA
Columbia, SC
23 June 2024

37427910R00065